By MARA PURL

Fiction
What The Heart Knows
Closer Than You Think
Child Secrets
Cause and Conscience
Nobody's Fault
Christmas Angels

Non-Fiction
Act Right – a Manual
for the On-Camera Actor
(with Erin Gray)
S.T.A.R –Student Theatre & Radio
High School Curriculum
S.T.A.R –Student Theatre & Radio
College Curriculum
Kenneth Leventhal & Co. –
A History of the Firm

Plays
Dracula's Last Tour
Mary Shelley –
In Her Own Words
(with Sydney Swire)

Screenplays & Teleplays
The Meridian Factor
(with Verne Nobles)
Welcome to Milford-Haven
(with Katherine Shirek Doughtie)
Guiding Light

Radio Dramas
Milford-Haven, U.S.A.
(100 episodes)
Green Valley
Haven Ten

S.T.A.R. Television Drama
Only A Test

S.T.A.R. Radio Dramas
Ashton Valley
Caught in a Web
Changes
Cruising
Deep Freeze
Fountain Hills Mall
Friendz
Frozen Hearts
Going Somewhere
In or Out
K-RAP
Love Child
Love Resolutions
San Feliz
The Curse of Santa Florita
The Peak Mystery
Toxicity
Westland High
Wrong Way

Mara Purl

What the
Heart Knows

Book One
The Milford-Haven Novels

Haven Books

Milford-Haven
PUBLISHING, RECORDING & BROADCASTING HISTORY
This book is based upon the original radio drama Milford-Haven ©1987 by Mara Purl, Library of Congress numbers SR188828, SR190790, SR194010; and upon the original radio drama Milford-Haven, U.S.A. ©1992 by Mara Purl, Library of Congress number SR232-483, which was broadcast by the British Broadcasting Company's BBC Radio 5 Network, and which is also currently in release in audio formats as Milford-Haven, U.S.A. ©1992 by Mara Purl. Portions of this material also appear on the Milford-Haven Web Site, http://www.milfordhaven.com
© *by Mara Purl. All rights reserved.*
Copyright © 1997 by Mara Purl Library of Congress Txu-766-374
Copyright © 2005 by Mara Purl, Revised Edition
No part of this book may be reproduced or transmitted in any form or by any means, electronic or mechanical, including photocopying, recording, or by any information storage and retrieval system, without permission in writing from the publisher. For information address: Haven Books
10153 ½ Riverside Drive, Suite 629, North Hollywood, CA 91602
www.havenbooks.net
Front Cover – Milford-Haven Cover Art by Warren Talcott
©*1987 by Milford-Haven Enterprises*
Back Cover – Milford-Haven Logo Art by Caren Pert Pearson
©*1987 by Milford-Haven Enterprises.*
Copy Editor: Vicki Werkley. Photo Credits:
Back cover photo by Lesley Bohm. Back page photo by Al Giddings

Purl, Mara.
  What the heart knows / Mara Purl -- 2nd ed.

  p. ; cm. -- (Milford-Haven novels ; Book one)
  ISBN-10: 1-58436-001-1
  ISBN-13: 978-1-58436-001-8

1. Coasts--California--Fiction. 2. Murder--Fiction. 3. Man-woman relationships--Fiction. 4. Coastal ecology--California--Fiction. 5. Real estate development--California--Fiction. 6. Petroleum industry and trade--California--Fiction. 7. Mystery fiction. I. Title.

PS3566.U75 W45 2005
813.6   2005928633

Library of Congress Control Number 2005928633

Published in the United States of America
First Edition 1997. Second Edition 2005.
Printed on 30% recycled stock.

This book is dedicated to the towns of Cambria, California, and Milford Haven, Wales, whose people, history, and geography have given to me bountifully of their riches. May their precious environmental beauty be forever unpolluted and unspoiled.

Acknowledgments

The New Edition

Welcome to this new edition of *What the Heart Knows*—what I like to call the *real* edition of my first novel. Nothing could be more exciting to an author than word from her publisher that new editions are planned for her entire novel series! The news is still just as thrilling, though in this case the author is an active participant in the plan. Why the new editions? So many reasons.... Because I'm a better writer now, because the first versions were part of our test-marketing phase, because these books were born in radio-land and had to put down roots in order to bloom in publishing-land, because in this changing world of independent publishing I *get* to do what most authors would give anything to do: rewrite their earlier works. And what made that possible in the case of this particular book has been the opportunity to work with my brilliant editor, Vicki Hessel Werkley.

What do the new editions contain? New segments, polished scenes, tantalizing clues that will pay off even better, now, in later books. And—the same favorite characters and complex twists of plot and of fate.

What do the new editions look like? Gloriously clad in new full-color covers, which are an uncanny metaphor for the process contained in their books. Layered, as are my stories, they begin with the original pen-and-ink drawings created for each book, then come into focus as that very piece springs into full color. It makes me feel I'm springing into full color too.

At Haven Books it's a brave new world as independent press marketing continues to evolve dynamically. My profound thanks to Peggy McColl for her launch-wisdom, abundance-thinking and soulful generosity; and to Randy Gilbert for sharing his Internet savvy. Special thanks to Lauren Tyson for heroic marketing, for sharing the spirit of adventure, for tireless energy and supportive enthusiasm. Thanks to Cynthia Johnson for marketing wisdom and high-flying creativity. And thanks to all the generous friends and colleagues who are contributing bonus gifts for my launches, all of whom are listed in the end pages.

The Original Edition

From a writing perspective, the first version of this book was an adaptation of scripts into a fledgling version of narrative.

One person who "got" what I was doing when most didn't, was my mentor Louis L'Amour, who believed in my project and told me to keep going with it. For encouragement and friendship my forever thanks to Louis, to Kathy L'Amour and to Beau L'Amour.

The other two people who always got it were my parents. Thanks to Père who introduced me to Shakespeare and to Dickens. Thanks to Mom who always believed I should be writing.

From a publishing perspective, the learning curve was steep while Haven Books made its first steps as an independent press. Thanks to the Haven crew: Reya Patton for foolhardy faith; Joyce Seed for marketing, book signings, and much more; Bill Leahy for expert printing and constant faith; and Sam Summerlin for all the meetings.

The Radio Drama

Milford-Haven had its first air date in 1987, and my thanks go to KOTR, in Cambria, California, our first radio home. In its next incarnation *Milford-Haven, U.S.A.* was broadcast on the BBC, for what I thank Ms. Pat Ewing, Director of Radio 5—a maverick network that launched a maverick show, and celebrated with us when we reached 4.5 million listeners.

And now at last we have the beginning stages of Internet Radio, and *Milford-Haven, U.S.A.* found an immediate home on www.yesterdayusa.com, created and run by the incomparable Bill Bragg.

Before there were any shows to broadcast, there were the cast members, and my thanks go to both the original cast of *Milford-Haven* and to the cast of *Milford-Haven, U.S.A.*, seasoned professionals who brought my characters so vividly to life that their work is inextricably woven into the fabric of the characters themselves.

Before there were cast members to record, there had to be a studio, and my thanks go to Engineer Bill Berkuta whose Afterhours Recording Company became our studio home, a workshop in which we created one hundred episodes of the first show and sixty of the second, and where we now create audio books of the novels.

Thanks to the late great David L. Krebs, our foley master, a gifted sound artist who created our aural reality. Thanks to Marilyn Harris and Mark Wolfram, who composed the haunting *Milford-Haven* theme and all the music cues which supported the emotional ebb and flow of the story. Thanks to Warren Talcott for the intriguing *Milford-Haven* poster, and to Caren Pearson for the compelling *Milford-Haven* logo art—each of which gave our town its visual reality.

And before there was a *Milford-Haven*, there was a young woman who had always lived in cities—Tokyo, New York, Los Angeles. I spent a summer performing in a play at Jim and Olga Buckley's Pewter Plough Playhouse in Cambria, and became fascinated with the life in and of a small town. With Elaine Traxel Evans's help, I immersed myself in this new culture—admittedly seeing it through the eyes of an environmentalist—and began to realize that it was not only a local drama that was being played out in its quiet streets, but a universal one as well.

Listeners in the U.S. and in the U.K. agreed, writing to me about their own lives, their own towns, and the commonality of the situations we face globally. My thanks go to my listeners everywhere. Several years later the link with listeners was to be vividly demonstrated, when the original Milford Haven in Wales embraced me as an honorary citizen and showed me those same streets, those same dramas, uncannily alike in the multi-cultural parallel universes we all inhabit. Thanks to Bruce Henrickson of the Belhaven House Hotel. Special thanks to Jim and Anne Hughes, who shared my vision even before we met, who welcomed me into their home, and with whom I continue to forge a unique town-to-town relationship.

My thanks go to my family and friends—helpful, discerning and, above all, supportive—Ray Purl, Marshie Purl, Linda Purl, Larry Norfleet, Erin Gray, Caren Pearson, Kathy Doughtie, Vickie and Bob Zoellner.

And finally my thanks go to my characters, among whom are—Jack, Zack, Miranda, Cornelius, Samantha, Rune, Meredith, Connie, Rick, Emily, Kevin, Joseph, Sally, Tony, Zelda, Notes, Susan and Cynthia, who are building, buying, painting, observing, planning, rehearsing, flirting, traveling, dealing, reporting, cogitating, dominating, dishing, healing, conniving, playing, sneaking and seducing, respectively.

Dear Reader,

The *Milford-Haven Novels* are an unusual form of fiction—serial novels. This form honors the roots of the original story that was first developed as a weekly serial radio drama. And these novels reopen the long-deserted trail blazed by Charles Dickens, whose lengthy, complex tales first appeared as serialized installments.

All writers grow and develop and come to know the depth of their own characters in the process. Though you may read these books out of sequence, I think you'll enjoy them most reading them in order, as I wrote them.

What The Heart Knows is the first book of twelve, and there are short stories that will continue to augment the story as well.

In future novels in the series, we will leave Milford-Haven to follow Miranda to destinations that fascinate her painter's eye and her restless heart. This novel takes her—and you—into the nooks and crannies of her adopted hometown, revealing some of its secrets and giving you a glimpse into its warm heart.

For it is the issues of the heart I'm exploring here: do we listen mostly to the head and ignore the rich, contextual information that beats steadily within us?

As the story unfolds, follow my footsteps over the interconnected pathways of those who inhabit Milford-Haven, and come to know what the heart knows.

Mara Purl

Milford-Haven

What The Heart Knows

Nestled between the pines and the ocean, and tucked away from any major metropolis, is Milford-Haven— an artists' retreat, a nature lovers' haven, a tourists' dream, and for some, just hometown U.S.A. Hardly the spot for a hotbed of controversy. Or is it?

What matters is not what gossip reports, nor what reason suspects, but what the heart knows.

— from Samantha Hugo's Journal

Prologue

It was completely dark in the unfinished house. To make matters worse, it was a moonless night, and such stars as normally sparkled in the clear, windswept autumn air were obscured by cloud cover.

Chris shifted her foot. She'd been standing in one place long enough that the sensation of the nail under her sole had numbed. She noticed it only when she moved. Still she waited, hoping her eyes would make a further adjustment to the unrelieved darkness.

Her pulse wouldn't settle. A hundred feet below, the sea pounded. An October storm was traveling the South Pacific, and even this far north, the Central Coast was feeling the effects. "Generating winds of up to 50 miles per hour...." she could hear her KSB-TV colleague saying. The house seemed to sway with the crashing surf, unsteady on its poles. That was an illusion, she knew. It was her own legs that were unsteady. She cursed him again, and her own insatiable curiosity.

Chilled in the cold structure, she pulled her jacket closer and tried to focus. She stood in what would undoubtedly be the living room—an expanse of white Sheetrock for the moment, which gave way on one side to a wall of glass. The view would be spectacular. On the opposite wall, flagstone had been fashioned into an oversized fireplace. It seemed curiously complete in this incomplete room, except for the rectangular hole gaping in front of it that left room for a hearthstone.

Imported marble, she remembered: one detail that had shown up on both sets of plans. Detail. Remember, she thought to herself, one detail can save your life. Reed had always told her that, and he was the best reporter in the business. She should leave this place, this swaying, unhallowed structure, menacing in its protruding metal shards and ragged concrete edges. But she'd been led here, vectored here by one clue after another. She had to find out.

A snap of fabric yanked her from her thoughts and sent her heartrate racing. As she held her breath, it sounded again. Like an exhalation, plastic wrapped over vacant window openings was sucked and pulled against the tape holding it to the framework. *Just the wind,* she reassured herself. The house itself was breathing, trying to expel its bad humors.

Chris took a step and her knee buckled. She caught herself by bracing against a cinderblock wall, tearing a piece of skin from her palm. She cursed in the dark, but the jab of pain had served to sharpen her attention.

The reasons she'd come here began to return to her mind in an orderly progression. He'd called her again. He'd been right about the plans. Chances are he was right about this house. Her own research had confirmed part of what he'd said, this illusive informer—a man with no name who called with tantalizing fragments of information. She tried to fit them together like so many shards of broken crystal, clear and sharp-edged.

She was here to gather more shards and she found herself resenting it. Joseph would be waiting with a clandestine dinner for two, all the more romantic for the secrecy. The thought hastened her, and she tried again to focus on the incomplete room. Clicking on her flashlight, she began inspecting the raw beams and Sheetrock.

"A171" was scrawled on one beam. "A172" was on the next. *Okay, so these guys can count*, she thought. On the next beam was an arrow pointing down. She knelt awkwardly, trying to read the next mark. It seemed to be a depth marker, followed by another arrow pointing down.

She'd have to check the length measurements printed on the poles. That meant climbing down the unfinished stairs into that black hole. Blacker than the unfinished, moonless living room. Cursing again, she began walking towards the fireplace, remembering to avoid the gaping hole in front of it.   Somehow through the wind and crashing surf, she heard a noise. Clicking off her flashlight, she hugged her body close to the Sheetrock. *I'm alone in a windswept rattletrap of raw beams and rusty metal scraps, and I ought to be home doing my nails*, she found herself thinking. Details. They were always her best defense against fear.

Clicking her flashlight back on, she began to search for stairs. There was nothing, however, but a ladder leading down into the hearth-well. "It's nothing but a black hole," she said out loud. "Blacker than a black cat's ass on black velvet."

"There's a quick way down there, Ms. Christian."

"Uh! Oh, for heaven's sake, you just about scared the.... What the hell are you doing here?" Her heart pounded louder than the surf. She clutched her flashlight and tried to keep it from bouncing across the man's features.

"I work here, Ms. Christian." The voice was steady, self-assured. The seamed face towered over a hulking physique.

"Oh...yes. I remember. Good thing you're here, because I could really use some help." A laugh erupted out of her throat like a burst of static from a malfunctioning radio. "You see, I've been trying to get a reading on these beams, and it's so hard to see in the dark." The man said nothing. She wondered how long the uninterrupted stream of words could surround her like a force field. "Say, you didn't even bring a flashlight."

"Very observant," he said simply.

"Guess you know the house real well if you work here. One of the construction crew, huh?"

"Right again."

"Well, listen, it's really getting late, and I'll come back in the morning when I can see better. Thanks a lot for all your help." She made a move away from the hearth-well, but it only brought her closer to the man. She could smell alcohol on his breath as he spoke. *Probably a bourbon drinker*, she thought, unable to stop cataloguing details.

"Oh, I haven't done anything yet."

"But you're about to, am I right?"

"Too right."

Humor had always been her strong point. That and clear, simple logic. *How many times have I played out this scenario in my head? How many times have I talked my way out of a tight spot?*

It was now or never, she knew. He might be bigger, stronger, more massive, but maneuverability was on her side. She clicked off her flashlight and hurled it at him. She'd already chosen exactly where her foot would land when she cleared the hole. In the sudden blackness she knew she'd have a second's worth of advantage. It was just the second she needed.

She heard the crack first, before she felt the impact. *Sounded like a gunshot*, she thought. And the next sound she heard was someone's voice, as though from a great distance. *It's yelling. No, it's screaming...screaming for help!*

As she landed, the wind was forced from her body like exhaust from a jet engine. That voice, she found herself thinking. *It sounds familiar... it sounds like mine. But it can't be. It's too far away.*

It'd been too many seconds since air had found its way into her lungs, and with a sudden clarity, she realized she wasn't breathing. In the same moment, Chris began to feel dirt pressing on her chest. Desperately, she inhaled, but she found no oxygen. Only the wet, sandy soil of the Central Coast.

Introduction

They came here from the plains to find the pine trees. They came here from the mountains to find the ocean. They came here from the cities to find serenity. They found all this, and much, much more in Milford-Haven....

Chapter 1

J ack Sawyer's alarm clock sputtered into life, its plastic frame cracked from abuse. A heavy hand swept down and banged the "snooze" button, then retreated under the covers.

Jack hadn't slept well. Keeping one step ahead of town, county, and state regulations didn't usually keep him up at night. But now he had to contend with Samantha. No matter what he did, he could never seem to get away from that woman.

He swung his legs out from under the blanket and didn't notice its long-forgotten coffee stains. He focused for a moment on the clock's digital display. The last digit no longer illuminated, so it was always a guess. He hoped it was still within a minute or two of 7 a.m.

Jack headed down the hall, his bare feet leaving an occasional imprint in the dusty floor. It would start soon—the phone calls from contractors trying to pick his brains; the messages from prospects who said other contractors could outbid him; the idiotic questions from incompetent workers; the nasty notices from inspectors. But today held the promise of a new client.

A sudden fit of coughing seized him, loud enough that he missed the first two rings of his phone, and on the third one his answering machine picked up.

"This is Jack Sawyer. I'm out. Leave a message if you expect me to call you back." He paid no attention to his own gravelly voice on the outgoing message. But after the beep, when an authoritative female voice began speaking, Jack started coughing again.

"Jack, this is Sam calling." As if he didn't know. *"If you've already gone to your office, you'll arrive just in time to get your two-hour notice. You're facing an injunction. Have a nice day."*

K evin loved the mornings better than any other time of day. In autumn, it was still dark and chilly when he got up. He never knew whether the sky would look pink or orange or lavender, so it was always a surprise. He liked that best of all.

The view from Kevin's porch raced down a steep incline through a stand of tall California pines. The smallness of the house was made up for by the size of the trees, which stood on protected land, so they'd never be cut down. The first rays of light penetrated the upper branches like the strobe lights of a *National Geographic* photographer.

Kevin's squirrel walked gingerly on the railing of the porch, chattering for his morning nut. Today it would be a cashew, and Kevin couldn't decide whether his squirrel was demanding an early Halloween treat, or stocking up for winter.

Kevin only had a few minutes before he had to leave for work. He liked to get there before Mr. Sawyer and make sure the coffee was made. It sometimes seemed to make Mr. Sawyer's mood a little better.

"Hey, little fella." He spoke quietly so as not to scare the squirrel off. "Want another one?" he wondered. He also wondered why it was always so much easier to talk to animals than it was to talk to people.

The doors at the Sawyer Construction Company were still locked and early-morning sunlight slid past decade-old layers of dust on the Venetian blinds. There was no sign of life until the light on the office answering machine illuminated, and the cassette tape began to squeal softly while it turned. Samantha Hugo was leaving nothing to chance.

Jack's voice crackled over the speaker. The professional message did nothing to belay the gruff impatience which set the tone at his office. *"You've reached the Sawyer Construction Company. We're out of the office at the moment, but leave your name, number and a brief message, and we'll get back to you shortly. Wait for the beep."*

"Jack, it's Samantha. I read in the paper this morning that you've announced the start of construction on that shopping center." Not even the filtering of the tiny speaker on his machine could make her voice small. *"You know perfectly well the plans have not yet been approved by the Planning Commission. I'd advise you to call me the minute you get to your office."*

B y the time Jack reached the Sawyer Construction Company he'd recovered from his cough and was ready to attack. He took the stairs two at a time and marched through the outer office without so much as a glance in either direction. Kevin knew better than to interrupt him.

Playing back the message Samantha'd promised would greet him at the office, nothing grated on him more than her voice—unless it was her tone. She'd *advise* him? He used the added charge of annoyance for fuel, and dialed her number even as the message played.

She answered on the first ring. "It's Jack, Samantha." Giving her no time to get a word in, he continued, "I figured you'd call. Had time to digest your morning grapefruit yet? Or was it prunes? I forget." There were certain advantages to having lived with the woman.

"I'm not going to let you ruin a perfectly good morning," she answered. "And by the way, I'm not about to let you ruin another perfectly good hill either."

"Oh, really?" said Jack. "And who do you think makes the decisions at this company?"

"Well, if it were me, you'd adhere to the Environmental Planning Commission's rules." Samantha'd always been one for rules. That'd been their problem in the first place. "You know Jack, you act as though Sawyer Construction enjoyed some sort of exemption. That's not how it works."

Jack's chair squeaked as he swivelled to face out the window, still spattered from last year's rainy season. "If you knew the slightest thing about how it works you wouldn't try to implement these rules, which only serve to block badly needed pieces of development, much desired by the community at large."

As far as Jack was concerned, it was simple. He'd come to terms with it years ago, and in the battle of idealism versus practicality, there was no question which had won. If you didn't have jobs, nothing else really mattered.

Samantha droned on. "Development is one thing, Jack. Ravaging the land is something else. I warned you to put a hold on this until our environmental impact study was complete."

"And I *warned* you what would happen if you ever tried to interfere with my business again. Let me see if I can shed a little light on rules for you. The rule, you said, was that no one was to know. You moved to Milford-Haven seven years ago, and I've obeyed your rule all this time, despite—"

"Despite what, Jack?"

His fist hit his well-worn desk. "— despite the fact that you continue to do everything you can to interfere with my business, every time I turn around!"

"I'm not trying to interfere with your business. I'm simply trying to do my job. Why do you insist on taking this personally?"

"Personally? There's nothing more personal to me than my business, and you'd understand that if you'd ever stuck with anything long enough to actually let it grow into something."

As Jack's voice continued to rise, from beyond his closed door, Kevin could hear Jack's side of the conversation with increasing clarity. He considered turning on the office radio to mask the sound, but then thought that might only annoy Jack further.

"Don't forget that your precious job is a political appointment."

"That was uncalled for, Jack, and I resent it."

At last she fell silent. He'd gotten to her. Jack shifted his weight back into his chair, allowed it to squeak long and loud, and lifted his feet, crossing them on his desk. Jack heard Samantha take a deep breath.

"All right Jack. What do you want?"

He spoke quietly, almost pleasantly. "I want you to stop

the investigation of that land. I want this shopping center to be unencumbered and unobstructed." It was the old argument. They'd had it hundreds of times before, on hundreds of proposed projects.

"You know I can't promise that, Jack. It's out of my hands."

"Fine. It's out of my hands too."

"What's out of your —"

"What's out of my hands is exactly when and under what circumstances the town of Milford-Haven finds out you're the former Mrs. Jack Sawyer." He started to laugh in spite of himself, and then decided the laughing felt better than anything had in a long time.

"What could you possibly stand to gain by doing this?"

She was grasping at straws. Jack could barely talk now through the laughter. "More to the point, what could you stand to lose?" His laugh was hard enough now that it began to turn into his cough. Not even that deterred him, nor diminished his delight.

"Jack! Jack!"

He hung up the phone with a satisfying click, and allowed his coughing to crescendo until it became a shout. "Kevin!" The door opened almost immediately. Just as he thought, Kevin had been listening to every word.

"Yes sir, Mr. Sawyer?" Jack was smiling, and Kevin wasn't sure he liked that.

"Get the windows cleaned. They're filthy."

Chapter 2

O ff-season, the tourist shops were still closed at this hour, and there was almost no traffic on Main Street, except for locals who were early risers looking for a good breakfast, and all of them had parked in front of the same establishment. In the row of windows facing the street, miniature pumpkins marched along window sills and cotton curtains with a tiny floral print were pinched into ruffles along brass rods hung mid-way down the panes. From the outside a passerby could see the tops of heads, but not patrons' faces. This was the only concession to privacy observed at Sally's, where the owner herself felt that any word spoken in her restaurant might as well have been spoken to her.

Inside, Sally's was a bustle of activity, as it usually was by 7 a.m. In the kitchen, the fourth batch of biscuits was coming out of the professional-sized stainless steel oven, eggs flew on and off the griddle at record speed, and June was starting another pot of coffee.

Out front at the well-worn counter, old Mr. Hargraves folded his newspaper and gave himself a startle as he elbowed his neighbor on the next stool—a straw man wearing overalls and a corncob pipe. As Sally served her customer a heaping plate of steaming grits and eggs over-easy, he complained, "Can't get used to Mr. Hay, over here."

Squeezing herself between two chairs to take another order, Sally replied, "Jest somethin' we do in Arkansas, Mr. H. Don't pay him no never mind."

"Not sure he oughtta be smoking," Mr. Hargraves said to her back, then dug into his eggs.

The screen door squealed and slammed as it always did. Dishes and stainless steel flatware clattered pleasantly, and Sally's famous biscuits filled the room with an irresistible aroma as Jack plopped himself into a chair, with Kevin in tow.

"Well, good morning, folks. What'll it be, the usual?" asked Sally.

He'd known her for four years, and still Jack hadn't decided whether that Arkansas drawl was an annoyance or part of the attraction. "Yes, Sally, and bring some coffee right away, will you?"

"That sounds good." Kevin always agreed with whatever Jack ordered, sensing it was more important to please him than to please his own palate.

"And who-le whe-at toast?" It grated on Jack, how she drew out the words and mangled the natural vowel sounds.

"Right." Jack knew that Sally had committed this menu to memory long ago, yet her pencil remained poised above her pad.

She wet the lead with her tongue before she wrote down his answer. "And two eggs over hard?"

She always managed to make it sound like an aberration. Eggs over hard. Jack liked them that way. What business was it of anyone else's?

"That doesn't sound so good." Kevin's quiet interjection was out of character, and it drew a smile from Sally.

"And bacon cr-isp?" She was still scribbling.

Jack was tired of the redundancy. "Sally I did say that I'd

have the usual, didn't I? Have you ever known the usual to be something other than it usually is? And did I not ask you to bring some coffee *right away?*"

"Well, my word, Jack," she said, "there's no call for you to get all upset now. Just don't get yourself in an uproar, and I'll get it. I'll put your order right in. Consider it done!" Sally turned towards the kitchen, putting on a smile automatically, with the well-practiced professional calm of a person running a business. But it was old Mr. Hargraves's eye she caught. He gave Sally a knowing wink, and she walked away humming the little nondescript song she always sang to calm herself.

She was barely away from the table before Jack mumbled, "What's wrong with that girl?" It was a rhetorical question, one that he frequently voiced. But it masked his respect for the little slip of a woman who would let no one, not even him, push her around.

"Gee, Boss, nothing that I know of." As always, Kevin had taken literally what was intended literarily. Jack retorted less audibly than usual. "Yes, well, you wouldn't know what was wrong with the girl if she sent it to you in writing."

"What d'you say, Boss?"

Jack's life was full of miscommunications. In the case of Kevin, he cultivated them. It was a game he enjoyed playing, an indulgence he allowed himself—taking advantage of what the young man missed, and ultimately, he knew somewhere in the recesses of his mind, a means of placing blame, should he ever need to do so. Having chosen to be the big fish in the little pond, he'd found no worthy partner in this small town against whom to sharpen his wit, except for Samantha, and she...well, she wasn't the worthy opponent she fancied herself to be.

Someday, he knew, he might regret his word games for some reason, might get caught or embarrassed, but even then he was sure he'd talk his way out of it before Kevin realized what had happened. He tried it now.

"That girl, that friend of yours who works for Samantha Hugo at the Environmental Planning Commission? I need you to contact her."

"Oh, you mean Su —"

Jack cut him off. "I don't want to know her name. Just get her to keep tabs on this investigation of theirs. I don't want any surprises."

"Well, okay, Boss, but I'm not sure what you mean by keeping tabs." Kevin liked Susan. He didn't like the idea of hurting her in any way.

Jack took a sip of Sally's delicious coffee and let the burning sensation overpower his impatience. "It means you be sure to let me know the moment Samantha re-opens the investigation, because I have a little something prepared for the press."

"What's that, Boss?" asked Kevin dutifully.

"Oh, just a little marriage we used to have." Jack wiped the coffee from his mustache. It allowed him to conceal the smirk creeping over his face. The thought of getting back at Samantha so poetically was delicious.

"No kidding? You used to be married to Samantha?" Kevin asked the question just a little loud. Sally returned with their food.

"Well, here we are...eggs, toast, and for you some muffins. And how about a warm-up on those coffees?"

Jack was unsure whether he was more anxious to get Sally away from the table, or to get Kevin to be slightly less stupid. Either way, his impatience was mounting. "Yes, yes, thanks, and that's all."

He issued it like an order, which Sally didn't seem to have heard. "Let's see, how about some marmalade?"

"I said that would be all for now, Sally." Tension creased

the corners of his mouth.

"Right! Well, I'm right here if you need me." Sally hummed again as she hurried off to handle the next customer.

Digging into his eggs and biscuits voraciously, Jack allowed the first few bites to take the edge off his hunger. Calmer now, he remembered to admonish his over-eager employee. "Kevin, I expect you to keep this quiet about Samantha."

"Oh, okay, Boss." Kevin was ever so slowly dribbling honey onto one side of his biscuit, trying, meanwhile, to think why his boss wanted to keep his former marriage quiet. "So it's a surprise?"

Jack couldn't stand to watch the deliberate slowness of Kevin's work with the honey, and at Kevin's comment he choked down a laugh with a morsel of bacon. He washed down his last bite with a swallow of coffee. Once again wiping his mustache, he said "Yes, you could say that." He began to smile at the prospect of damaging that reputation Samantha held so dear. "In any case," Jack continued, enjoying the way the words felt in his mouth almost as much as he'd enjoyed Sally's home cooking, "it'll be common knowledge soon enough."

Zack Calvin enjoyed the drive up the coast with an abandon he'd been missing for a long time. Of course, there was the usual kind of escape back home in Santa Barbara—that's what Cynthia was good for. But this was different. He was his own man for the rest of the weekend, following no corporate schedule, no social calendar. For once, nothing was expected of him.

The 8 a.m. meeting in Los Angeles had gone well. As he'd pulled out of the parking structure, he'd allowed the canvas top of his Mercedes 500 SL to retract automatically and found himself impatient as usual to get out of L.A.'s Friday traffic. By the time the density of cars finally thinned out, he was passing through Thousand Oaks, and he pushed the pedal to the metal when he came around the big, gentle curve of Highway 101 in Ventura where the road finally touched the coastline.

Taking in the sparkling water and the jagged mountain lines where land's end continued to wander ahead of him, he took a deep breath and settled into the leather seat. An autumn haze softened the profiles of offshore oil rigs as they marched out from close to shore, and he found himself naming each of them, ticking off the construction dates and remembering some of the details of their histories.

But today was to be his day to leave the oil business behind and see how the rest of the world was getting along. Digging his heel a little more deeply into the car's plush carpeting, he nudged the speedometer a notch or two higher. Worried for a moment, he removed his sunglasses and scanned the road through his rearview mirror—sometimes a cop car was hard to spot with the sun low in the sky. But Zack's eyesight was as good as any Air Force pilot's, and he relaxed, realizing he'd seen merely a fellow traveler with wheels as fast as his own.

He didn't know exactly where he was going, or how long he'd drive. He decided to allow himself the ultimate luxury of unwinding even as his car wound up, and of seeing where he...wound up. The little joke made him laugh. A silly laugh, and a delighted one, at being able to think of anything so trivial.

Relieved not to be stopping in Santa Barbara, he continued north on 101 and sped past the San Marcos Pass, taking the long way where it followed the peninsula out into the Pacific, the languorous pace matching his mood. He wasn't hungry or tired of the drive by the time he was passing the turn off for Solvang. It was a cute little tourist town—almost too charming. All the buildings matched, and every brunch spot offered *aebleskivers*, the rounds of fried dough the Danes served with powdered sugar and jam—delicious, he had to admit. One had to be in a particular mood to enjoy Solvang, and today wasn't the day to play tourist.

Turning off at San Luis Obispo, charming college town that it was, he rode past telephone poles festooned with brightly colored posters, and glanced into coffee shops crammed with students exuberant with the fall-energy of a new semester. Even then he didn't stop, beckoned by an irresistible urge to travel California Highway 1.

The older, narrower road returned him to the coast, and he glided down the big hill toward Morro Bay. The highway contoured beautifully along the deep bay where, as a boy, he'd seen tankers standing off shore, as his father had explained the ways of the great ships. He thought of stopping. But pleasant though they were, the memories only coaxed him to go farther, away from all reminders of business. He almost stopped again when he saw the sign "Harmony. Population 18." But by the time he was considering it, he'd sped past the only access road, and Harmony slipped away in the late morning sun.

"Cambria" announced itself quietly, picture-postcards of streets and houses winking between trees, but the open road bypassed its center, and the one traffic light that might have stopped him remained a bright, beckoning green. A few miles later not even William Randolph Hearst's sumptuous estate tempted him, and he sped past the Castle. Within a few minutes, he entered the perimeter of Milford-Haven and knew this was what he'd been looking for.

Turning off the highway, he nosed into a main street that passed through a valley between hills. On the hills were perched tall pines, houses nestled among them. Parking in a diagonal spot outside a row of shops, he turned off the car engine and allowed himself a moment of silence before opening his door. Leaving the car's top down, he closed the door, stretched, and breathed deeply of ion-rich air, laden with the scent of pine and eucalyptus.

A whiff of sizzling meat wafted past Zack's nostrils, and he glanced up Main Street to discover its source. Instead of finding it, he found himself wandering from shop to shop, gradually realizing that each one housed original arts or crafts of some sort, and that he'd happened not so much into a tourist town as into an artists' colony. Every store's windows were decorated for the season—some with an autumn elegance, some with a whimsy of goblins and ghosts. Outside the local Chamber of Commerce, he took a map from the rack left for visitors.

Reading something about a gallery called "Finders'"" as he walked, he looked up in time to see he'd stopped directly by its front door. Walking in, he set off the pleasant sound of door chimes, and was greeted by a voice speaking in ya Montreal accent. "Good afternoon, Sir. May I 'elp you?"

"Oh. Thanks. I was just reading about your gallery here and I wanted to see it for myself."

"*C'est bien!* " Nicole had worked at Finders' for a year now, and her spiel was well rehearsed. "We represent a cross section of styles here, we have everything from nature to 'igh technology and from modern to realism...." As she continued to talk, Zack found himself processing the accented words: "ehv-rrreh-thing," "tech-no-lo-jee"...she was still talking. "Well, if I can explain anything to you about our artists, or their work, please do not 'esitate to ask. My name is Nicole." As she walked away, her heels clicked on the stone floor, and her hips swayed, confined chicly in a tightly fitted skirt.

"Okay thanks," he replied.

She turned around just in time to catch him looking, and smiled.

Zack lifted his gaze, returned the smile and said, "I'll just have a look around."

He was faintly aware of growing hungry, but enjoyed keeping the hunger at bay with the pleasant thought of discovering some delightful little lunch spot. His eye fell on a nice painting that had captured some of the local charm...pines, ocean, mist. Very restful....

He continued walking, realizing that the gallery was larger than it had seemed at first. Coming around a corner, he was stopped by what he saw.

The painting hung alone on the far wall—a window to another world, a lost world of primeval forest and untrodden seashore, a dreamscape where footsteps left no prints in a sun-dappled, sandy cove.

Zack stood transfixed, his breathing heavy and deep, color rising up his neck. As though mist from the painting might cool his face, he drifted closer to the canvas, and waited to receive its message. When none came, the rational mind tried to sort and categorize the fading familiarity. *This cove, I've seen it before...I just can't recall...maybe as a child? No, it doesn't look like Santa Barbara.*

What logic and memory couldn't explain, acquisition could solve. Even as Zack made his decision, he tried to explain it to himself. *It'll go right on my office wall...the ocean, those rocks, that magic cove....* Almost in a trance, he walked toward Nicole's sales desk. "Excuse me."

Her head was bowed over a file, the front lock of her short, smooth hair concealing her face. She looked up, sweeping her hair out of the way. "Yes, sir?"

"I've decided I'd like to buy one of your paintings." He could hardly believe he was saying it. "That one over there, with the cove and the beach."

"I see Monsieur is a man who decides quickly." Nicole had seen impulse buying on occasion, but this was quick even for an impulse.

"Well, yes I...I suppose I do. Is it available?"

"Let me just look it up in our catalogue," said Nicole, and she lifted a large leather-bound volume with plastic-covered sheets. She turned the pages carefully, her long, clear nails tracing color reproductions. "Ah." She'd found it. Even the likeness on the page made his urge strengthen. "This one is on loan from the artist. I'm afraid I'll have to get permission before—"

"Uh, look, I'm just up here for the weekend," Zack interrupted her, "and I'd like to be sure to settle this before I leave. Do you think you could put me in touch with the artist? I'd like to just call him myself." A strange anxiety gripped him at the thought of losing the painting.

"Actually, the artist is a woman, and she does not answer the studio phone between noon and 4 p.m., but since you're in a 'urry why not drop by her studio? Probably you could catch her either today or tomorrow...I do not think she would mind, in this case."

Slightly taken aback at the prospect of having to explain his sudden passion to the artist herself, he nonetheless overcame his hesitation. "All right...I'll do that."

Pulling some materials from the file drawer, Nicole drew her mouth to one side in a slight smile. " 'ere is a brochure about her work, and it 'as the address on the back."

Zack took the brochure, flipping to the back. For the second time that day, something stopped him. "She's a beauty!" The words burst out of him involuntarily, under his breath, at the sight of her picture.

"*Pardon, Monsieur?*" Nicole was busying herself with the package she was preparing for him, working meticulously.

"Oh, it's a beauty, that painting."

"Yes, sir." Nicole wasn't fooled. "Well, you go out the gallery front door, and turn left, and go up the 'ill...." She was giving him directions to the private studio of the artist, Miranda Jones.

Chapter 3

Cynthia Radcliffe stood in front of her full-length mirror and admired the view. Her hair was always a slightly different shade of blond, but this week was the best color yet, she decided. André had done a good job with the cut too—long enough to play with, and short enough to make a fashion statement.

Exactly what statement she was making with the dress was another matter, and the thought of Zackery's face when he saw her in it made her throw back her head and laugh. Whether it did more to emphasize the sculpted waist or the shapely breasts was hard to say. Either way, the strategically placed lace and the cling of the fabric would have the desired effect.

It hadn't taken long for Cynthia to decide on Zackery Calvin. And it had confirmed Santa Barbara as a logical choice too. It was far enough north of Los Angeles to be distinct from the complex and sordid layers that made up a large city. It was more like a politically correct suburb where the privileged could have the best of both worlds: driving into L.A. in two hours—less in the right car—yet comfortably removed.

She imagined there would be less competition in Santa Barbara as well. L.A. was full of sexy young blondes who could distract a man's attention. Of course they were drawn like moths to the flame of Hollywood, and spent their youths dreaming of stardom. Cynthia considered all that to be a colossal waste of time, and knew exactly where to focus: money and men.

So often the best of both could be found in the same place. And this was the most important thing about the beautiful and tasteful city of Santa Barbara. There was plenty of money here. So she knew she'd find powerful and successful men.

Zackery was certainly both. The amazing thing was that he was also young and handsome. It wasn't necessarily to her advantage. She'd generally found that older men were more stable professionally, and more needy emotionally. She'd had some success with such relationships, adding both to her personal fortune and to her reputation.

At first she'd singled out Mr. Calvin, senior as the most likely target. Rich. Widowed. High-powered CEO. But then Zackery had spotted her first. Since that would have spoiled it with the father, she'd decided to allow his advances. She hadn't yet admitted to herself that it was the last time she'd felt completely in control with Zackery.

I've got to make sure that everybody is there...make sure I haven't overlooked anyone.... she mused while adjusting her makeup. Cynthia had a gift for entertaining. It was in her nature to leave nothing to chance, and to trust no one else's ability to get things right.

I'd better call the printer.... She'd gone over the details endlessly, but one could never be too careful.

"Hello?" Mr. Dinzle had been a master printer for forty-five years and saw everything there was to see in black and white.

"Oh, yes, hello, this is Cynthia Radcliffe—with an 'e'." She'd read somewhere years ago that little idiosyncrasies made one more memorable, and had decided that adding the "e" to her name—and reminding people of the unusual spelling—would become one of her trademarks. By now it had become automatic.

"Oh, yes, hello, Miss Radcliffe. Are you calling about your invitations?"

"Yes. How do they look? Did the gold borders come out just perfectly?"

"Oh, yes, Miss Radcliffe, they did, and so did the little gold..." Mr. Dinzle paused, but didn't express his disapproval. "Uh...*hearts* you wanted on the outside of the envelopes."

"You don't think they look too...well, too...."

Ever the soul of discretion, he replied, "I'm not quite sure what you mean, Miss Radcliffe."

"Oh, well, after all, this is rather a too-too occasion, isn't it? And besides, nothing is too good for Zackery...."

She was going out on a limb further than she ever had with Zackery. For one thing, he seemed to have a strange ambivalence about parties, especially big ones. That didn't worry her too much, because after all, he went to them all the time. In fact, that's how they'd first met. Then again, this was different. It was a party in his honor.

"Well, you would know best, I'm sure," Mr. Dinzle continued. "Would you like me to read the invitation back to you?"

"Oh, yes, you'd better do that."

" 'You are cordially invited to join Mr. Zackery Calvin and Miss Cynthia Radcliffe—with an 'e'—in celebrating Mr. Calvin's birthday at a benefit for the Arts Museum, at the Calvin Estate'...."

Doing the party as a benefit had been a stroke of genius. Cynthia would congratulate herself again later, when she calmed down. For now she could feel the anxiety creep over her again. Everything had to be perfect. "And you got the address right?"

"Oh, yes, Miss Radcliffe."

"And it says black tie in the bottom corner?"

"Oh, of course, Miss Radcliffe. Blue tie in the corner."

Cynthia felt her throat begin to tighten. "Oh, no no no no no no!"

"Printer's joke, Miss Radcliffe."

She gulped air and tried to make a quick recovery. "Oh. How cute." She was still breathing hard. "Well, that's all for now, I guess. I'll send James down to pick them up, if I can't get there myself later." The Calvins' butler had agreed to help with the party, though he had not seemed enthusiastic.

"That'll be fine, Miss Radcliffe. Thank you."

At first Cynthia had considered waiting to have Zackery's party until she could afford to move into a better condo. She knew exactly what she wanted. The payments would be steep, but well worth it to establish herself in the right kind of neighborhood and create a space suitable for entertaining. She wanted a perfect setting for intimate dinner parties of which she could be the center of attention. She would have them catered, of course. But that would have to wait until cash flow was improved. And in any case, if she played her cards right, it would soon be a moot point.

Then she'd had the brilliant idea of making his party a museum benefit. This had enabled her to approach Joseph about the use of the house and grounds, and to earn a gold star for placing the Calvin philanthropy in the limelight. Immediately, the party had grown well beyond the bounds of intimacy.

I hope 500 invitations are enough. Two hundred are on the list so far...better invite about that many again...all the club members are already invited, and of course, the other major charities have been notified....

She sat quietly for a moment, and allowed herself to go into a daydream about the big event. She would have on the dress—just on the point of being too risque for the Santa Barbara intelligencia, but so tasteful that no one would be able to comment. The men would love it; the women would hate themselves. Zackery would spend the evening trying to concentrate on his guests, but unable to keep his eyes—or his thoughts—off her. She would present him with some stupendous gift in front of all his family and friends. They would dance to the sounds of....

"Oh, the music! Of course! I never got an answer from the orchestra!" She picked up the phone and began dialing frantically. "Oh, no, that's right, I asked James to call them for me, and he said he was already taking care of that." She hung up, took a deep breath and began to think she was smarter than she gave herself credit for.

Cynthia had never been a good student, except when she thought something might be relevant to her own goals. Throughout junior college those endless projects requiring research in the library had bored her to distraction. Certainly she'd never found newspapers to hold the slightest interest. But then she'd discovered the society pages—why had no one ever told her? Now she'd become a devotee.

She looked at the *Santa Barbara Register* thrown haphazardly on her bed, examined her nails wondering how badly the newsprint would smudge on her polish, and grabbed the paper. She hadn't read the Julia Cavendish column yet. Scanning the details of a Junior League luncheon in support of local artists to make sure all the names were familiar, she placed her fingernail on the page when she spotted a new one. "Zelda McIntyre," she read, "lawyer with her own Artists Representation firm, and she manages painters...."

Her mind began to click into gear. *I better get her to come to this or I'll have the museum mad at me....* She dialed directory assistance, got the number, and placed the call. An answering machine picked up.

"Hello, this is Zelda McIntyre at Artists' Representations.

We are out of the office at this time, but please leave a message and we will call you back."

By the time the machine beeped, Cynthia was prepared with her message. Looking down as she spoke, she held Zelda's name in view by pointing at it with her long, pink nail.

"Oh. Hello? Oh, hello, this is Zelda." Cynthia knew at once she'd said something wrong and looked up. "No, no no I mean of course, you are Zelda...I was looking at your name when I dialed.... Excuse me! This is Cynthia Radcliffe. You've probably heard that I'm co-hosting a Benefit for the new Arts Museum. I would like to send you an invitation so please get back to me and let me have your address. I'll talk to you soon. Oh! My number is 555-1040. Thank you so much! Bye-Bye!"

She hung up. Mercifully, the message-leaving ordeal was over, and Cynthia's dreams of a magical evening were well on their way to becoming reality.

Chapter 4

M iranda Jones loved the afternoon light. She always had, even as a child. She'd loved to sneak out of the house in the afternoon, sketch pad and crayons in hand, when she was supposed be taking a nap. She'd loved to climb the hill on the far side of the property and make picture after picture of the Northern California mountains before the sun sank into the ocean. That was one of the good memories.

Milford-Haven had only been home for three years, but there were days when it felt as though she'd lived here forever. It was the first place she'd put down roots of her own, and that had been more important to her than anything, except for her work. Perhaps it was because too much had been given to her, and she'd had to reject it in order to lay her hands on something the family couldn't provide. Perhaps it was because so much had been promised and so little delivered, in love and loyalty.

In any case, people here knew her only from what they saw of her and her canvases. There was no cumbersome history to get in the way of friendships which could be formed purely on their own merit. The smallness of the town was a constant delight to her, as was the fact that the citizens seemed to have at least some sense of the preciousness of their environment.

This was Miranda's real passion. What she could not bestow in daughterly affection to her parents, she freely and joyfully gave to strangers, making her paintings private prayers and public offerings. She went to any and every length to imbue her work with accuracy. If it meant hanging off the end of a cliff or traveling through treacherous country, she did it without so much as a heartbeat of hesitation. There was a quietness in her work, and a power. And after her dangerous travels, she always returned here to let that truth flow through the end of her paintbrush.

She'd chosen this apartment—actually the left side of a house—because of the large upstairs room. She'd known the moment she saw it that it would be her studio. With its wall of picture windows offering a panorama of the Central Coast, and ample room for her supplies, it was the most perfect work space she'd ever seen. She couldn't count the number of hours she'd stood here now, facing all that beauty, and her easel. Even the expanse of white canvas didn't scare her so much when that afternoon light turned everything to gold. It was why she never answered the studio phone at this time of day.

Today, however, the paintbrush twitched in her hand. Unable to do any real work, she moved to the built-in desk that ran the length of the windowed wall in her studio and picked up the stack of postcards. They featured her own miniature watercolor— one of the first non-wildlife pieces she'd done in quite a while.

The printer had done a good job, she decided. The color looked true, the proportion appealing. Main Street stretched away to the ocean, pines rose along the edges to touch a blue sky. It hadn't seemed complete till she printed the town's name in pale lettering like scripted clouds. And she hadn't been able to resist placing in the foreground the lovely gallery that handled her work.

She'd created the tiny painting and had it made into

postcards for practical purposes—letting people know about her work. She'd already sent them to her short list: a few friends, her always-supportive sister, her ever-skeptical parents, and of course Zelda, who'd help with a business contact list.

But there was something else about the postcards too. She liked the crisp edges and bright image, felt in it the vibrancy of the little place she now called home. Somehow the town had a heartbeat that matched her own, and the postcard took its pulse. If the universe had fulfilled a promise to her, this little card was her thank-you note.

The phone rang again. She stared at it, then decided to answer.

"Darling! It's me!"

Knowing the voice after the first syllable, Miranda said, "Hi, Zelda."

"Well, it's simply the most brilliant thing you've ever done. The postcard is sensational. I want you to send me a thousand immediately."

"A thousand? But I—"

"You have more marketing sense than you've ever let on, Miranda. This is going to turn the tide."

"I'm not sure I have the budget to—"

"We'll solve that in just a moment. By the way, what are you doing answering the phone?"

"What? Oh...I don't know. I don't seem to be able to paint anything today. I'm very distracted. I just have this feeling something is about to happen." Miranda had always had strong intuitions but was just beginning to trust them.

"Well, Miranda darling, it is! Now I have some good news and some bad news."

Miranda braced herself. "Bad news first."

Zelda launched into one of her long and detailed stories

about being unable to get the client to go for the "big" piece. Zelda never seemed clear on the actual titles of Miranda's works, but she must have been talking about "The Seals."

It wasn't like Miranda to worry about money—though there was never a surplus. There was, however, an "ordered chaos," according to her sister. It didn't seem chaotic to Miranda. The bills stayed in a neat stack until she sold a painting—then she paid them all. "I was counting on that income...I don't know how I'll make my payments now," she said absently.

"Didn't I tell you there was good news?"

"So you did."

"Well, darling I feel so dreadful about this, after promising I had this one all sewn up, that I've decided I'll buy it from you."

Miranda had an immediate and automatic aversion to loans of any kind. Her mother had found that out, but that'd been a long time ago. "Zelda, that's ridiculous. You can't afford to float me for $10,000."

"That's true. So I'm giving you $5000. And who said anything about floating? This is money for value received."

So it wouldn't be a loan. But it would be a mercy-sale. "I can't let you."

"I insist! I've already written the check, and I'm just about to put it in the mail. It will only take a day or two to reach you from Santa Barbara. And anyway, it's high time I had my most significant artist on conspicuous display in my own house."

Zelda seemed very certain of herself, and very sure this was something she should do. Something felt wrong about it, but Miranda pushed her doubts aside. This was her manager, and it was an offer that would meet her immediate needs. She hesitated one more moment and then yielded. "Uh...thank you, Zelda. Listen, I'm going to go. I don't want to run up your phone bill on top of everything you're doing for me."

"That's my girl. We'll talk soon. Ta ta!"

Miranda hung up the phone and tried to return to the afternoon light, still feeling the events of the day weren't through with her.

Zelda McIntyre had just turned fifty and was looking to broaden her horizons. She'd already made her fortune once, but was ready to do it again, this time perhaps sharing a bit less of it with an "ex."

Zelda had never been married—or so the revisionist version of her autobiography would read. In fact, she'd been married once for about ten minutes on the emotional clock, and had never had the slightest inclination to repeat the fiasco, unless she could find a true equal.

She'd been a plain-looking girl who'd grown into a handsome woman, and one who'd learned how to make use of her appearance. She'd learned to dress expensively. Her wardrobe of Chanel and Dior suits encompassed every fabric from spun silk to *crêpe de Chine*, every correct color starting with the power-red reserved for meetings, and her collection of couturier scarves was by now a signature.

The minute she'd graduated from the University of Cincinnati, Zelda—she wasn't called that then— had changed her name and moved as far away as possible. Ohio was such an ignominious place to come from that she did her best never to mention it. Los Angeles had seemed fairly distant geographically, but it was light years away morally, and therein lay its appeal.

When she'd first arrived she'd done museum work, but that had been laughable in the culturally deprived Los Angeles of the

1960s, and there seemed no point in pursuing it unless one were at the Met or the Modern in New York. Instead she found a way to combine and prey upon the best and the worst of L.A.—the extraordinary freedom of expression, which bred good artists, and the hunger for status and success, which corrupted artists and patrons alike. She became a corporate art consultant, first working with a fabulously intelligent and well-connected older man, and then, when she no longer needed her mentor, competing with him by opening her own firm.

Like so many things in the fast-paced and materialistic life of which she was the perfect exemplification, it was all about acquisition. What had once been the dignified pastime of the highly cultured, was now the competitive bidding war of the upwardly mobile. What collectors of yesteryear had taken years to amass, acquisitors of today expected to gather in days. And that was where Zelda came in.

Corporate Art Professionals was successful from day one, winning clients faster than Zelda could list them in her Rolodex. CAP was eventually successful enough to go public, but Zelda never wanted that, and kept the corporation tightly held. They placed over a million dollars in corporate art the second year, and continued up from there.

She'd gradually developed a stable of artists she liked working with regularly, and later branched into managing the careers of a few of the most promising. Miranda Jones's success as an artist had been no surprise. Zelda knew and trusted both her own eye, and her own ability to market a good product. What she hadn't counted on was liking the girl.

Zelda thought for a moment about their phone conversation. Miranda's concern had been almost touching. But Zelda seldom let that worry her. This was strictly business. As she thought about her next call, she flipped open her burgundy leather address book, and with a short, polished nail, scanned down the page for the number.

"Hello?" The man's voice was dignified, if a little strained.

"Oh, hello, Mr. Clarke?" She spoke with deliberate warmth. "It's Zelda McIntyre. I have wonderful news for you. I've been able to talk Miranda Jones down to $10,000."

There was no reply.

Before the silence grew too awkward Zelda continued. "Isn't it marvelous? Of course I know you're in Philadelphia, but I could leave the piece at your Santa Barbara office this afternoon." She knew when to close a sale. "Would that be convenient?"

"Yes. Fine."

"And you'll instruct your office to have the check ready?" These nasty little details might be unpleasant to some. Zelda didn't find them so.

"Yes," said Clarke. "Should the check be made out to you?"

"Yes, it can be made out to me."

"It'll be ready."

"Good. Well, it's a pleasure doing business with you, Mr. Clarke."

There was again no reply, except for the click of Mr. Clarke's phone. But Zelda was unperturbed. She hung up the dead phone. It was just that simple, if you knew what you were doing. And what poor little Miranda didn't know couldn't possibly hurt her. Zelda would pick up the check for $10,000, send $5,000 to Miranda, and make a nice little deposit at her bank. She would just see to it that Miranda and Mr. Clarke never met.

Zelda sat back in her plush office chair and ruminated over the events of the day. Miranda was happy. Mr. Clarke was happy. And for herself, well, she was working on it. She had a long way to go before her plans came completely into focus.

She thought again about Miranda for a moment, and about the bond she'd felt when they first met. Miranda was strong, in a different way than she was, but perhaps for some of the same reasons. She would never talk about her past— another thing they shared. One thing they did not share was this zeal for the environment, which Zelda considered merely to be the latest fad of anachronistic hippies. She did not, however, fail to recognize that "environment" was beginning to heat up as a marketable buzz word in the world of art.

Zelda thought for a moment about the girl's sincerity. Such concerns were washed away, however, by the image of that dreadful painting. *I wouldn't be caught dead with a painting of seals in my living room,* she thought. *In fact, maybe with some of my new profit, I'll get myself a seal coat!* And with that thought, Zelda leaned forward in her chair, and began to laugh.

Chapter 5

T he Belhaven Inn," Nicole had said in her Montreal accent. "It is not so much for the tourists, *vous comprenez?* I t'ink you will like it." Grateful for the recommendation, Zack headed for the little strip of beach, saw the inviting hand-carved sign and pulled into the parking area. Pumpkins and gourds decorated its small porch. But with its seasoned wood, blue and white paint, and cobblestone walkway, the motel could have been in Nantucket or Monterey, Nova Scotia or Wales.

Opening the front door, Zack was greeted by a whiff of aromatic pipe smoke, a gas fireplace, and the lilting tones of the proprietor. "Afternoon," said a gray-haired gentleman. "Looking for a room, are you?"

"Yes." Zack wasn't sure of the man's accent, but it sounded Irish. "Have one available?"

Looking over the top of his glasses, the gentleman said, "Oh, indeed we have," then busied himself with providing a sign-in card for his new guest.

"This will be your key, then, and we do hope you'll be enjoying your stay."

Turning the key of Number 5, Zack opened the door,

allowing orange light from the late afternoon sun to flood the room. Feeling curiously at home, Zack tossed his duffle on a chair and looked around. A carved armoire housed a TV, but he closed the doors to hide the intruding device. The rest of the furniture, carved to match, was gleaming pine, worn and well-used.

Glancing through a tourist guide, he noted several of the restaurants he'd passed in his walk through town, including the one where he'd had a delicious bowl of soup for lunch. Later, the prospect of another simple, honest meal was a pleasant one. With no agenda to meet, he opted for a brief nap before dinner, and as he stretched out on the wide bed with its thick comforter, Zack looked forward to a peaceful evening.

Looking forward—that was something he almost never did. Everything was always *now* in his life. Over-scheduled professionally, in personal matters he always acted on impulse, rarely allowing himself the luxury of anticipation.

Yet here he was, with delicious deliberation, choosing delay over immediacy. Tomorrow, he'd look for the beautiful artist and her compelling painting. For today, he'd allow himself to feel the pull of the painting, and have something to look forward to. And with that thought, the pounding waves and the fresh sea air wafting in through the open window lulled him into a light, peaceful sleep.

The sinking sun had left its final traces of mulberry, marine and indigo across a blackening horizon. The colors matched the bruise on Susan's arm perfectly, and she touched the yellowing center of the uneven, concentric rings wondering how much longer it would hurt.

She didn't really mind the bruise. It was earned in a good

cause—dancing too close to that guitarist, who'd swung the neck vehemently and connected with her just below the shoulder.

Tired from another day of battling both Samantha and the polluters of the planet, she threw off her clothes and pulled on her favorite Halloween nightshirt, its fading white skeleton standing out against the black cotton.

Bunching the pillows on her unmade bed, she had one more task before turning in for the night. Under the light of a bare bulb, Susan opened her book of clippings. Leaning on one elbow, she turned the pages carefully, tracking the progress of the bands who toured the Central Coast.

Leather-clad and pierced, tattooed and spiked, they stuck out their tongues at fans and screamed their passions to microphones. She loved every defiant gesture, but in the brief moments before she fell asleep, she had a mission to complete. Certain she'd seen the same face lurking in the background at more than one local concert, she had to find out who he was.

Can't see a damn thing, she said out loud. She couldn't use that language in front of Samantha, but her posters didn't mind. Scrambling off the bed impatiently, she found an old shoe box on her makeshift desk and rummaged through it. Retrieving a dusty magnifying glass, she blew on it, and held it close to the pages.

There—a man with dark hair...hard to make out the face...the image was nothing more than a collection of dots, now that she could see it close up. Still, the way he stood, the line of his jaw...she recognized him. He was there at every concert.

She continued looking to see if she could uncover a clearer photo of him. There! He was standing between members of *Topic*. *Oh my God, oh my God...who is he who is he?*

Reading each of the names, she counted bodies, correlating names to faces. The fourth from the left. "Rune Sierra." *Gotcha. Next concert...I'll find you.*

It was something to dream about.

Night had fallen in Milford-Haven, but it never fell dark enough for Jack Sawyer to feel completely unworried. He had for some time felt uneasy about Sally, but he still hadn't come up with a logical reason for not seeing her. Much as he found her demeanor in the restaurant a bit overbearing each morning, still she was discreet. And somehow she concealed more down-home good sense and feminine essence behind that apron than most women managed to reveal in a black evening gown.

Sally knew how to play the game, and he liked that. Southern women were smart when it came to men. They generally didn't try to prove their intellectual superiority the way northern women—or even those from northern California—did.

She'd arrived unobserved, parked in the back, and had made herself as comfortable in his kitchen as she would have in her own. Dinner had been superb as usual. "Oh, this is nothin' but a little fried chicken and taters," she'd said, spooning that delicious gravy into a cradle of the smoothest mashed potatoes he'd ever tasted. She was good. She knew it. She made no fuss about it.

She'd kept him at bay while she cooked, slipping out from under his embraces with little giggles and excuses about getting himself burned. But it was after dinner now, and he knew she was expecting him to make his move.

"Well," she said. It sounded more like "wail." "Shall we have some coffee in the livin' room?" He thought about coffee for a moment, and knew it would be good. But already he had a taste for something else. He pushed himself back from the table, the chair making a loud scraping noise on the hardwood floor. Sally looked up, slightly startled. The faintly alarmed look in her eyes was the spark of inspiration he needed. He stood quickly, while she busied herself with silverware. He moved with surprising agility for a man his size. In one step he stood behind her. His arm circled her waist, and he lifted her off the floor.

She gasped as he took her past the sofa and past the kitchen. "Jack," she spoke with difficulty, "just hold your horses now." He chuckled at her quaint little expression. "Jack, couldn't I even take off my apron?"

By then they were in the bedroom. He threw himself backwards onto the bed, still holding her against him. "Oooh!" Sally was winded by the fall, and they both began to laugh. "Yes, you can take off your apron, Sally." He kept his voice low and seductive, a rasping whisper that tickled her ear, his tone both inviting and menacing. He saw that it scared her slightly, even as it pushed her over the edge into passion.

He got up and stood over her. Sally lay on the bed looking up at him, waiting. He stared into her eyes while he removed his clothes, then started on hers. The apron sash untied easily. Sally said nothing, submitting to the moment, and to the man.

She closed her eyes. "Jack, Jack...." she murmured softly. To Jack it sounded almost like "Jake," but he liked the sound of it. She threw her head back now, and he could see she was enjoying herself. It excited him further, and he could no longer contain himself. She held him, understanding, if not sharing, the intensity. And then Jack fell into an immediate and heavy sleep.

His lovemaking had been gruff, but rhythmic. She clutched a corner of the sheet and tried to see his face in the darkened room. By the angled light of a street lamp she could see his bureau. That single box still rested on top of it. No pictures. No knickknacks.

She lay there wondering how long she could continue breathing under Jack's weight, and yet she hated to wake him. She remembered the first time she'd slept with him, how she hadn't felt the weight of a man in so long she'd almost forgotten the sensation, and had welcomed even the discomfort of it.

After a few minutes he stirred. She looked so soft, staring up at him, her eyes moist and full of meaning. Sally was the closest thing to tenderness he'd felt in twenty years, and it reassured him that those qualities were still there. He didn't think about it for long. He rolled off her, and they each drifted into sleep, lost in their separate thoughts.

It was still dark when Sally woke with the automatic alarm that went off in her head whether she wanted it to or not. She lay there for a few minutes, looking up at the ceiling and considering how little her personal relationship with Jack had affected his life. She thought about the addition onto her restaurant he always promised to build, and how his work on her building might cause more of an emotional investment than their physical intimacy had. But even that project, she was beginning to admit, was becoming nothing more than a remote possibility.

Knowing by now it must be 5 a.m., she slipped slowly out from under Jack's worn comforter. She padded quietly around the end of the bed, pausing at the bureau, and at the dusty box. An almost overwhelming desire to open it swept over her, and she glanced at Jack who was still snoring undisturbed. Her fingers touched the edge of the box's hinged top, and she began to lift it carefully. Suddenly there was the explosive sound of Jack's cough, and Sally allowed the box's top to fall, as she jerked her hand away. Her heart beating fast, she took a step to the edge of the bed and reached for the robe lost in the folds of the comforter.

"Ooww!" she yelped. While her attention was focused on retrieving the robe, Jack slipped his hand out from under the covers and gave her a good slap on the behind. He snapped the light on to get a better look at her. "Ja-a-ck," she said. His name became a three syllable word. She scowled at him and smoother her tousled hair. Twisting the belt tighter around his enormous robe, she turned and marched down the hall.

She'd be in and out of the shower before he got out of bed. The woman was diligent about getting the restaurant open on time. Jack never knew whether he slapped her like that to wake himself from the pleasant stupor of love, or to teach her not to get used to kindness. Either way, it brought him back to reality—the reality of Jack Sawyer, who needed no one.

Chapter 6

W ind rose off still-dark water, scudded across waves, lifted over bluffs and rustled through trees, carrying the scent of ocean and pine into Miranda's bedroom. She inhaled the aromas into her sleep where they blended with her dream.

A canopy of stars sparkled overhead through a perfect circle of tall, sheltering branches. *Where am I?* A high, protected place, waves lapping below, perfect stillness arcing overhead. A safe place that welcomed and understood.

Yes, this is the place.

Long ago—as long ago as childhood—she had written the words: *where mountains meet ocean, where art meets science, where heart meets heart.* Later in her teenage diary, she'd drawn three pictures: a mountain at the edge of a sea; the moon reflected in a well; two overlapping hearts. Even then, she'd known someday the drawings would become paintings.

She'd captured the mountain-ocean image first, earth contours rising to a sculpted ridge, then plunging into the sea, tall pines spearing up from the bluff, boulders anchored offshore.

Then there'd been that unplanned drive south. She'd happened upon the very coastal profile she'd envisioned, the place choosing her as much as she'd chosen it. It had drawn her to her new home, to Milford-Haven. Within the year, she'd moved.

The voices of reason had objected. *If you want to be an artist, go to New York, not to some out-of-the-way place where no one will ever discover you.*

But the heart knew.

No one had understood why she had to leave. She'd come anyway.

In a sense she'd painted her new home into existence, imagined it so clearly it had emerged from the infinite beyond and taken tangible form.

But here, now, this high, windswept place—it was new. It was one of the places she had yet to paint. This was an introduction, then, a flight forward in time or space, a preview reserved for this dream from which she didn't want to wake.

Wind caressed her cheek, riffled her hair. And then, she was in his embrace.

I thought I was alone here. A moment of disorientation, surprise. *Of course, this would be a shared place.* Soul answered soul, acquainting itself with what was already familiar.

A shiver followed the trace of his hand up the smooth, cool skin of her back, under her arm, into the warmth between her breasts. He whispered her name as he bent over her, his lips tickling her ear. She smiled in the dark, inhaled the scent of pine that clung to his skin. Long legs slipped between hers, the muscles of his arms lowering him slowly till his weight began to press, chest to chest, a steady thrumming, heart to heart.

Two overlapping hearts.

His voice spoke her name. *Miranda!* Insistent, it demanded recognition, recollection, realization. *Miranda....* Tender, it called forth appetite, ardor, aperture.

Heat flushed over her skin, sang in her womb.

Then it was his heat, his mouth taking hers and her responding, her heart moved in her chest as he pressed himself to her, hers the depth that captured the brilliance of his heat, burning like a bright moon.

The moon reflected in a well

Light crashed against her eyes, and they flew open to blink against dazzling sunshine spilling over the windowsill. Suddenly aware of weight pressing on her chest, she was startled to realize it was her cat.

"Shadow?"

"Meow."

Miranda's hand crept from beneath the covers to caress the kitty's head. "Were you trying to wake me up?"

Shadow purred a contented reply.

I was dreaming something. What was it?

Whatever it was, it was gone now. Miranda stared into the amber eyes of her cat and contemplated the wilder feline she would soon be painting.

With the light especially beautiful this morning—more gold than usual—Miranda was taking full advantage. Going into a state of intense concentration, she refocused on the day she'd originally photographed the cheetah, and the specific moment when it'd looked at her. Caught in the flow of her work, she had no sensation of when the paintbrush was touching the canvas, and when it was not. For all intents and purposes, she was not in the room to hear the phone ring.

Her answering machine picked up. The volume was turned down. *"Hello, this is Miranda. I'm busy painting so please leave me a message. Thanks."*

The machine beeped. *"Miranda, this is Sam. I know you're in your studio painting. Listen, I uh, I'd really like to talk. If you can take a break for a few minutes, just meet me at Sally's at ten."*

Miranda continued painting, vaguely aware that something mechanical had clicked in the background.

Miranda paused and rotated her shoulders. She had no idea how long she'd been standing in one position. She did a *Tai Chi* brush-knee movement and shifted her weight. After two more rotations, she put her paintbrush in the jar of water and stared absently out the window. Switching to acrylic paint had been part of her desire to get away from toxic chemicals, but the paint had presented her with a whole new series of challenges. It didn't behave like oils, and she missed the control. She was satisfied, however, with having gained one more measure of control over pollution.

Out of the corner of her eye, she saw the light blinking on her answering machine and registered that someone had called. Listening to the message, she was torn when she heard it was Samantha. The painting was pulling at her, as it had for weeks. But so was the slight edge of urgency in Sam's voice. Despite their age difference, they'd become good friends. Miranda walked to the bedroom, grabbed a sweater, ran a brush through her long hair, and headed for her garage.

She never locked her bicycle to anything, and seldom closed the garage door. It was one of the things she loved about living in Milford-Haven—that she didn't have to. Reminding herself to shop for some goodies for trick-or-treaters, she picked up her helmet and hesitated. She should put it on. Instead, she fastened it to her handlebars, mounted the bike, and rolled out the driveway. As she headed down the winding hill towards Sally's, the wind caught her hair and she found herself smiling as she always did, enjoying the effortless cruise to the bottom, and even looking forward to the long pump back to the top later.

Sally's was bustling, and a glance through the windows would have yielded nothing distinguishable from any other morning, except for the stranger sitting at the counter.

"Can I get you one of those?" Sally asked him as she came out of the kitchen.

"One of what?" The man snapped at her, his tension as obvious to her as if he'd been wearing a sign.

"Well, I see you've been staring right at my fabulous, gooey cinnamon sticky buns. They're famous, you know. You can have one while you're waitin'."

"Waiting?" The man was all suspicion and no charm. Sally poured him some coffee.

"Young lady's made you a mite nervous."

The man was stunned by her presumption, and even more stunned when she continued.

"What's her name? Maybe I know her."

His finger stopped tapping the counter top. "Chris Christian," he clipped.

"Chris Christian." Sally elongated the vowels almost beyond recognition. "Nope. Not one o' my regulars."

Sally looked over the man's shoulder just in time to see a glare in her direction. *Well, getaway*, she thought. *That Samantha's got her patience stretched tight as a pig-bladder balloon.* Sally glanced down at the man's coffee cup. "You let me know when you're ready ta order." Turning her slight body sideways, Sally scooted between tables and disappeared into the kitchen.

Outside, Miranda pulled her bike to a stop and leaned it against the window boxes in front. Opening the screen door, she winced as it banged shut behind her, and she promised herself for the hundredth time not to let it happen again.

"Over here Miranda!" Samantha waved from the corner table. As Miranda approached, Sam continued, "You got my message. Sorry to interrupt your work. I usually don't call you in the morning but I— "

"I know you don't." Miranda thought she looked worried. "That's why I figured it was probably something important." She'd carried her helmet in, and she hung it on the back of her chair, then in a fluid motion angled her body between chair and table to sit down.

As Miranda sat, Samantha tried to decide where to begin. "I uh, well...." Much as Samantha wanted to talk this out, it was not going to be easy. She'd kept it to herself for year after year. "Something's happened, and because of it, I'll have to make a decision."

Miranda looked up sharply at her friend. "A decision about what?" She didn't hear Sally approach.

"Ah, decisions, decisions. Crumb cake or carrot cake, right?"

Sally looked a little tired today, Miranda thought, and there was a vulnerability behind her usual strength. "Hi, Sally." Miranda always enjoyed seeing her, and would have liked to chat, but it was Samantha who needed her attention. "Um, how about two coffees to start with. If that's okay with you, Sam?"

"Yes, fine." She sounded curt, even more so than she

usually did with Sally, Miranda thought, and wondered again if there was anything she could do to bring these two friends of hers to some sort of mutual appreciation.

Miranda knew Sally could never resist overhearing a juicy tidbit of gossip, and sure enough Sally stood there humming her nondescript little song, her pencil hovering over her pad. "Sally, we're not going to order anything else right now."

"Oh, right! I just got my pen stuck in my apron." Sally hummed as she walked toward the bank of coffee pots.

Miranda chuckled, and then refocused her attention on Samantha.

Sighing, Sam started. "You know that Jack and I were married years ago."

Miranda nodded. "Hard to imagine you with Jack Sawyer. It's almost funny in fact. Is he holding this over your head in some way?"

Samantha sighed. "Oh, yes, every few months he trots out our previous marriage as a threat to my reputation. And naturally he wants me to curtail investigating his latest building project."

"Well, obviously you're not about to do that. You're the head of the Environmental Planning Commission. He can't touch you."

"I'm not so sure," Sam countered. "My job is a political appointment, as he is always quick to remind me."

"If it's your job you're concerned about, do you think that in this day and age people really care about a divorce that happened over twenty years ago?" Miranda usually drank tea, but was looking forward to the taste of Sally's coffee. Samantha still seemed worried.

"No, I don't think they'll hang me for that, but there's something else you don't know about. No one knows."

"Here you go, girls." The coffee smelled delicious. "No

one knows what?"

Sally's timing was too good. Miranda decided to cover, before Samantha got annoyed. "No one knows what big ears Sally O'Mally has. Thanks for the coffee. Mmm, this smells great."

"How about one of my fabulous, gooey cinnamon sticky buns? Sinfully tempting, if I do say so myself."

"Just coffee is fine, Sally." Samantha's voice was cool.

"Still trying to watch your figure Samantha?"

Miranda glared at Sally.

"Oh, you know me. I never can resist a joke." Sally walked away from their table.

Samantha looked at her retreating back. "Honestly that woman is insuffer —"

Miranda cut her off. "Sam, what were you going to tell me?"

Samantha sighed again and lowered her voice. "I was going to say there was more to that marriage than even Jack knows. We had a child."

Stunned, Miranda sat in silence for a moment. Now that Samantha had started to talk, the story began to tumble out. "When we decided to get divorced, I was already pregnant, but I didn't realize it at the time. After I found out, I let the divorce go forward."

"And you had the baby?"

"He...he was with me...less than two years. I had to put him up for adoption and...it's haunted me for years...I've never really known if I did the right thing...."

"You must have been very young."

"I...I don't mean to burden you with all this, Miranda." Sam glanced around the room. "What concerns me now is that between my job being so visible, and Jack making these threats more and more frequently, some zealous reporter might start digging into my past. And it's not only me who might be affected by it."

Miranda nodded. "It's the child." They looked at each other for a moment, considering the facts.

"He's a grown man by now, with a life of his own," said Samantha quietly. She looked down. "And he has no knowledge of his connection to me. There would be no way for him to know."

Staring into their coffee cups, neither of them heard Sally approach. "No way for who to know what? I swear you girls have the most fascinatin' conversations."

Miranda was acutely aware that this wasn't the moment for Sally's humor, nor for her nosiness. It seemed the right time to make a move. "Sam, maybe we could—"

"Yes, I have to go, too." Samantha was already on her feet. "I have a meeting in a few minutes." She and Miranda left a dollar apiece on the table and headed more quickly than usual for the door.

Looking back over her shoulder, Miranda called, "Bye, Sally!"

Sally looked toward them and called out a quick, "Bye-Bye!"

Miranda pushed the screen door open, its spring rasping as always. "Sam, give me a call after your meeting." Her friend seemed drawn and tense.

"I will, Miranda." They hugged. "Thanks."

Back inside, Sally was still standing by their table. She continued looking at the spot where they'd stood, with the professional smile frozen on her face. She took a moment to think. *Oh, yes, you do have interestin' conversations, she said to herself. Sometimes my eavesdroppin' is too good. So. Jack is a daddy!*

She could sense every feeling she had for Jack realigning. She trusted him less...why had he never told her of his marriage? Yet she understood him better...a man with even more of a past than she'd thought. She was shaken, right down to her sensible shoes.

Samantha had always annoyed her, with her dynamism, a wit that sailed over Sally's head, and a tall, statuesque beauty she herself could never aspire to. And she was a redhead. Sally'd never trusted redheads. Samantha had a lot to lose if Jack undermined her reputation. And Samantha had played it cool for a long time.

But of the two women, it was Sally who'd played it coolest of all. And of the two, it was Sally who had the most to gain from this information—and the most to lose.

Chapter 7

Jack leaned one hand heavily on his desk. The bitter brew in the bottom of his cup was left over from morning, and a waxy residue had formed over its surface. Jack hoisted the stained mug to his lips, and a drop of cold coffee rolled down his mustache, dropping onto the Lambert house plans. "Look, Kevin, I said I want that wall taken out of there. That's what the client wants, and that's what I want." His steely blue eyes bored into Kevin, who, as always, tried to explain himself.

"Okay, Boss, but I was just following these regulations over here. It says 'A wall shall not be removed between two —' "

Jack stood up so abruptly the remaining coffee in his cup sloshed out and splattered onto the already-stained hardwood floor. "I don't care what it says in some stupid rule book. I've been a successful builder for thirty-two years, and I know what I'm doing." He'd spoken rapid-fire, but now he spoke slowly and deliberately. "Are you going to trust some book or are you going to do what your employer tells you to do?"

Kevin paused. "I guess I'll do what you tell me to do. After all, you're the boss and everything."

"And everything." Jack added an emphasis which

transformed Kevin's benign expression into one weighted with double-entendre. "What's the date that inspector said he'd be taking a look at the Smothers property?"

Eager to please, Kevin rustled through the closest stack of papers and was grateful when he came up with the right one. "Uh, let's see...the eleventh."

Jack looked past Kevin, fixing his eyes on some invisible spot on the opposing wall, as he often did when he began to cogitate. He calculated the number of days required before foundation piles could be driven. They'd be in by the eleventh. The inspector would have no way to check their depth. Jack lifted the corners of his mouth in a slight smile, which his mustache concealed perfectly.

"So, Boss, we'll have to let him check the depth on those before—" Kevin could think only in terms of honesty, and since that was all he knew, it was all he expected of others. The sound of the phone ringing interrupted his train of thought. "I'll get it out there, Boss." He hurried out of Jack's office.

Jack called after him. "You go on with your work, Kevin. I'll get the phone." He cleared his throat for a moment, then picked up. "Sawyer Construction."

"Mr. Sawyer? This is Russell Clarke."

"Oh, hello, Mr. Clarke."

"I assume you were expecting my call." It was already 4 p.m. in California. Headquartered in Philadelphia, Clarke was calling after hours....unless he'd already started traveling west.

"Yes, I've been looking forward to hearing from you." Changes to the original design were the most enervating part of the construction business. But Jack knew better than to alienate an important client. He tried to sound reassuring and pleasant, a technique he'd all but lost. "So, what have you decided?"

"Let me ask you this—" There was a rustling as Clarke covered the receiver to speak with someone else, with whom Clarke was apparently consulting. Feeling awkward and annoyed, Jack waited until Clarke finally asked, "Will you commit to the figure you gave me for the changes?"

"Yes," Jack answered quickly. " I will stand by my estimate." "In that case," Clarke said without hesitation, "we have an agreement."

"Excellent. We'll get started. And I look forward to meeting with you when you come up from Santa Barbara."

"Yes, I'll be in Santa Barbara briefly for a business meeting, and will drive directly to Milford-Haven."

Standing rapidly, he kept a tight rein on his voice. "Very good. See you then." Jack hung up, the exuberance of closing a deal beginning to surge. Yet there was something about Clarke, something he couldn't control, and it made him uneasy.

Kevin came back into Jack's office. Seeing the smile, he asked, "Was that the inspector? He said he'll go ahead and measure first?"

"No, no that was Clarke, that new client, and he says he wants to go ahead with the new house. I don't know why he calls it a house—the place is going to be a mansion. And it'll have the price tag to go with it."

Kevin knew this should be good news. He also recalled comments his boss had made when Mr. Clarke first presented the rough ideas for his house. "But, Boss, I thought you said you couldn't build it to code with the design he wanted."

"That's not a problem."

Kevin's instinct was to question Mr. Sawyer further, not to be argumentative, which was not his nature, but from a deep desire to understand how something could be true one day, but not true the next. "It isn't? Well, how come?"

Jack took a long moment to look at Kevin, his thoughts far beyond the technicalities that were stumbling blocks to his employee's straight forward way of thinking. "There's more than one way to build a house, Kevin. The longer you work for me, the more you'll realize that."

It would still be light out for hours, but to Sally it felt like shutters and bye-bye. These childhood phrases surfaced unobstructed when she was tired, or when she spoke with Mama. She remembered every detail of the farm in Arkansas. She remembered Mama closing the shutters at night. *Come on, Sally girl. Shutters and bye-bye,* Mama would say. *Time to go to sleep.*

Sally glanced back into the restaurant. The chairs were upended on the tables, the overhead lights were out, the coffee warmers turned off—all set for tomorrow morning. She went into her private office and pushed the door closed a little too hard. The sound of it slamming was satisfying. But it was nothing compared to the satisfaction of taking off her shoes.

At moments like this, Sally indulged the luxury of talking to herself. "Aaahhh, that feels good. My poor little toes all squished up in those shoes all day.... Boy, has it been a long one." She didn't know exactly who she was addressing. Nor did she imagine how much loneliness she was trying to keep at bay.

She began humming again, the tuneless tune that filled the air with noise—in itself, company of a sort. She reached for her diary. It was another of her rituals. She had no illusions that she would do great things one day, which should therefore be recorded. She did, however, know that with no one to be her confidant, she'd either have to write things down, or bust.

For some time, Jack had been a sore point and she hadn't known what to do about it. He ate her meals night and day. Daytime in public. Nighttime in private. That seemed exciting at first, and wise. No need to broadcast a relationship that might or might not take. But after three years, it had surely taken.

And yet no one knew about them, knew they were a couple. He never took her anywhere anymore. Two summers ago they'd laughed and flirted at the county fair. Last summer they'd gone to Morro Bay for a boat ride and a romantic dinner. She could still remember the scent of the salt air on his skin.

Sally loved to build. She'd built her business, her life in a new town, her relationships with customers. There was nothing she liked better. Except building something together. She'd seen it in Jack the first time she'd gone to his office. He was strong. He knew how to build.

She'd bought the building partly on the strength of his carpentry estimate. After he'd put in the counters she needed, they'd talked about adding on a room. The addition. Always they'd talked about the addition. He'd promised. Promised to build it for her. Day after day, month after month went by, and the completed plans gathered dust.

And today, today he'd hurt her. She'd always known he had a past. That was part of what made any man interesting. But this! This was more than one of his stinging slaps. This was a blow.

She began writing. *It was pretty hard not being noticed but I managed to overhear Jack talking to Kevin about the fact that he used to be married to Samantha. Jack married to Samantha! Imagine that! He never told me. He just never told me. I guess he never really tells me nothin'!* Pausing a moment, she wiped a hot tear from the corner of her eye.

Anger began to rise in her, pushing in waves against the sadness and disappointment, like a competing tide. Guilt would intrude later, like a terrible undertow. But now, the anger was winning. *Today I think I found out how to get the addition built.*

I've been waiting for this long enough.

Sally slipped the journal back into its hiding place and pushed in her desk drawer with a satisfying slam.

Chapter 8

Miranda stood staring out the windows of her studio, lost in thought. It'd almost emerged—the lighting on the distant hills in Kenya that she was trying to remember. Once she could see it in her mind, she could get it onto the canvas. But now it was gone again, as though she were looking through a pair of binoculars she couldn't quite focus.

Still distracted by this morning's conversation with Sam, on one level she was intrigued at the thought of parent and child being forever lost to each other. What would it be like to be unencumbered by the pressures of parental expectations? Shaking her head as if to rid herself of such callous thoughts, she remembered her friend's sadness. She stood in front of her canvas, trying to force her attention to return to her work.

The sound of her doorbell startled her. It seldom rang unless she was expecting someone. She turned away from the window and started out of her studio without really considering whether or not she wanted a visitor.

Still trying to think about the lighting in Kenya, she opened the door and was surprised to see a stranger standing there. "Yes?" she tried to sound pleasant.

"Oh, hello, I didn't mean to disturb you. I see you've got your painting clothes on."

Without thinking, Miranda looked down at her overalls, then blushed at her own foolishness. Afraid the man would say, "Made you look!" she said defensively, "Well, I usually do." When he continued to stare, she asked, "What can I do for you?"

"I came about one of your paintings, the large one that's hanging in the Finders' Gallery."

Momentarily distracted by trying to remember which piece he was referring to, Miranda stood there mentally flashing through her canvases as though she were looking at color slides. The man shifted his weight, and it suddenly seemed rude to keep him standing outside. "Uh...would you...like to come in?" Standing aside to let him pass, she closed the door, and then felt awkward at having let this stranger into her house. It was another thing that struck her as ridiculous—her own knee-jerk politesse that was too deeply ingrained to overcome. She remembered being five years old, covered with measles. When the doctor had asked her how she was, she'd automatically answered, "Fine."

The man smiled. "I was at the gallery yesterday, and they said I'd find you in your studio. I'm uh, I'm Zack Calvin." He extended his hand. "And you're Miranda Jones."

"Miranda Jones...." she said it simultaneously with him, and smiled. Still in the handshake, she stared into blue eyes until she began to feel self-conscious.

As Miranda withdrew her hand, Zack was the first to recover from the silence. "Great place you've got here." He took in the large sunny room comprising a living room, dining area, kitchen and foyer, with every space nicely defined, but each completely open to the rest.

"Thanks," she said, self-conscious again. "I love it here in Milford-Haven. It's peaceful enough to get some work done, and beautiful enough to have something to paint all the time." *What am I, a travelogue?* she thought. *I sound like a brochure.*

"When I saw your painting at the gallery, I...I really want to buy it."

"You...you want to buy it...just like that?"

"Just like that. What do I have to do?" Zack felt the words gather weight, as though he were talking about more than the purchase of a painting. He stared at Miranda, aware he was making her uncomfortable.

"Nicole at the gallery sets the prices on all the work they sell. Besides, that one really isn't for sale. It's kind of a special one to me, and I lent it to Nicole for the gallery because she was so insistent...."

"Not nearly as insistent as I can be."

Miranda looked at him for a moment. "You go after what you want, don't you?" *That's something Meredith would say.* Her sister was the assertive one. It felt good for the first instant, but then she chafed in the aftermath, feeling brazen.

"Yeah, that's what they tell me. Listen, do you have time to knock off work for a while?

"Knock off?"

"We could go to the gallery and complete the sale. And besides, I don't know anything about Milford-Haven. I just came up here from Santa Barbara for the weekend. Maybe you could show me around a little?"

"Oh, I've got so much to do, I really shouldn't." *The man oozes charm.* She could hear her sister commenting as though she stood across the room. In spite of herself, Miranda began to smile. "On the other hand, I wasn't getting much done, and maybe a walk would do me good...."

Zack was smiling back. "That cove in your painting—is it around here?"

"Why, yes. That's...that's a great place to start." *Start what?* she wondered. "I have brushes to put away, paint tubes to close. Can you give me a few minutes, I— "

"Of course," he interrupted her. "I'll wait right here."

"Okay! I'll be as quick as I can." Miranda spun, then, stopping herself, she called back, "Um...have a seat. Or...no, would you like some juice, some—?

"I'm fine!" Zack called to her. "Take your time!"

Darting across the large, open room into her studio, she replaced the caps on the open tubes of paint, hardly registering the unfinished painting on her easel. Then she rushed down the stairs to her bedroom, suddenly wondering if she looked even slightly presentable. She was landing hard on each step as she ran. *I probably sound like a herd of elephants*, she thought, *or like the fat boarding school girl I once was.* She hit the bottom step and raced into her bathroom.

With a nervous energy, she ran a brush through her hair and glanced at her face in the mirror. Her phone rang, and she realized—too late—that she didn't have to answer it. By then, she'd said hello.

"Darling, I've found you in again!"

Zelda had uncanny timing. Not necessarily good or bad. But uncanny. "Oh, Zelda, hi. Listen I only have a moment. Someone's waiting for me."

"Darling, you sound so excited. Who is this person? He must really be something to take you away from your work. It is a *he*, I trust?"

"Yes, Zelda, it's a *he*."

"Oh, little Miranda gets a social life." Zelda teased like a Portuguese Man-Of-War, floating innocently on the surface, stingers ready just below the water line.

"He's interested in my work, Zelda, and he's standing in

my foyer. I have to go."

"You've let him into your house? A man you don't know? My, he must have made quite an impression. Where's he from?"

"He's from Santa Barbara."

"Well, if he's *anybody*, I must know him."

Perhaps if she told Zelda the vitals, she could get her off the phone. "His name is Zack Calvin, and I would say from his manners that he's from a good family. He hasn't told me where he works. Is that what you wanted to know?"

"Sounds secretive."

"Zelda, we've hardly had a chance to talk! I think he wants to buy a painting."

"Oh. Well, in that case, I'll let you go, dear. I'll call you back."

"I know you will!" Miranda hung up. As she raced to change her clothes, she thought about the stranger waiting in her living room.

I f she'd had an extra bike, she'd have lent it to Zack for their trip to the Cove. As it was, they drove there in his Mercedes, and she felt awkward and ridiculous for the second time that day. The discomfort was taking her out of the moment, something that seldom happened. *What am I doing? Leaving the studio in the middle of work, climbing into the ostentatious car of some rich stranger? Did he do this all the time, seduce women by trying to buy their paintings?*

The car bristled with gadgets and buttons she didn't understand. It looked like the interior of the Space Shuttle, and she'd be at a loss if she suddenly had to drive such a vehicle. The leather seats offended her. So, she was sure, would the gas consumption, if she could ever find the gauge in the instrument array.

A strand of her long hair escaped from its barrette, drawn by the wind, and she tried to recapture it while looking for the Hearst Castle sign. Lost in her anxieties, she nearly missed the turnoff, but motioned just in time, and Zack slowed the sleek gun-metal gray beast into the Santa Carlita Cove & Wildlife Sanctuary parking lot. A long, sickle-shaped eucalyptus leaf drifted down from the high trees overhead, and landed on the windshield. It was Miranda's first good luck sign of the day. Suddenly cheered by this small token, she re-entered present time as though she'd been given a gift.

Miranda bounded out of the car before Zack could open the door for her. "If you have some hiking boots you might want to put them on," she said, and started down the path to the beach.

"Boots?" Zack called after her, "at the beach?"

"The beach is only the first part of the walk!" Miranda called back to him. There was something mischievous in her remark, and Zack smiled, realizing he'd have to hurry to catch up.

A few moments later, Zack had strapped on hiking boots and taken off after her. The path crested over a small hill, and as he came up over it, the glimpse of the Cove stopped him in his tracks. He knew from having seen Miranda's painting that there was something magically appealing about the place. But he was altogether unprepared for the effect it was having on him.

Miranda was by now a small figure, receding farther into the landscape. She turned toward him, waving him on. Zack registered the fact, but was unable to uproot himself from the spot. He knew he'd never been here before, so it couldn't be a memory. Yet seeing the perfect spot, he seemed to be experiencing *dejà vu*, moving through the scenery as if it were a dreamscape.

With effort, Zack lifted his feet, and began trudging his heavy boots in the sand. He waved at Miranda, who then turned to face the incoming tides. The floor of the Cove was perfectly flat, and curved outward, lapped by the gentle waves of a small bay. Above it rose a cliff that formed a peninsula jutting out into the ocean, a forest of tall trees running along its heights.

Where they'd entered at the south border, the hill was small. But at the north border—which she'd had now almost reached—the cliff rose three hundred feet off the sandy floor, making the Cove at once both cozy and dramatic.

Zack attempted to run the rest of the way, and found it exhausting, the sand pulling at the treads in his soles. The effort seemed to clear his head, though, so he persisted until he finally stood beside Miranda, panting. She smiled at him. "Ready to start climbing?" she asked. There was that mischievous twinkle again.

Climb what? Zack wanted to say. But "Sure" was the only word that escaped with an exhale and, without catching his breath, he began pursuing her as she walked straight toward the back wall of the Cove.

The wall seemed to be just that—perhaps not the smooth cement of a fortress, but treacherous nonetheless with dirt rutted by mud slides and only the occasional tree root for footing. It seemed a foolhardy mission, and Zack had trouble believing that anyone had successfully scaled this previously. But upon closer examination, the thread of a trail appeared, and Miranda planted her feet along it with an expertise that must have come with practice, Zack decided, as his own feet lost traction intermittently.

When they finally made their ascent, they were met with a barbed wire fence, placed so close to the edge of the cliff that Zack could get no more than a toehold. Teetering, he waited speechlessly as Miranda tested the pegs holding the fence in place. Finding a loose one, she lifted it, and ducked under the barbs in a fluid move, motioning Zack to do the same. He imagined himself rolling over backwards and sliding all the way back to the beach, but managed to get himself under the wire with only a minor snag in his shirt.

When Zack stood, he found he was in a forest of eucalyptus. He looked over at Miranda, who stood with her eyes closed, inhaling deeply. "What is this place?" Zack asked.

"Shhh," Miranda replied. She walked over to him then, and whispered, "This is what the locals call the Enchanted Forest." And with that, she began walking softly on the blanket of fallen leaves. Zack followed, still slightly winded, but intrigued. Where they were going from here he couldn't imagine, but he was beginning to let go of his worries about it.

Miranda touched his sleeve. She pointed upward, and when he looked he saw they'd moved into a different forest altogether, this one of tall pines. Tall wasn't quite the word. The trees soared upward a hundred feet, giving the forest a mythic proportion. Although the Cove had been sunny, mist was hanging in the upper branches, and as they watched, an owl winged by overhead, hooting a greeting—or a warning.

Miranda led on through an obstacle course of felled trees, majestic even in their demise—huge root systems exposed, standing taller than two men. She picked up a pine cone the size of a pineapple—an exquisitely detailed wood sculpture.

And then the forest changed again, and Zack found he was following her, hunched over, scratching his way through a bramble of low pines whose underbrush arced away in covered corridors. When he managed to look up, Miranda was nowhere to be seen. He felt as though he were playing a sophisticated game of hide-and-seek, terrified of losing sight of her, too proud to call her name.

He pressed on through the brush, his shirt a total loss by now, just trying to keep the sharp branches from his face. And in the next moment, he gasped, reeled, and clutched at the nearest tree trunk. The path, such as it was, had ended abruptly and Zack found himself at the edge of the peninsula, looking straight down at a three-hundred foot drop to a beachless, rocky coastline.

Having recovered his bearings, Zack let go his stranglehold on the tree trunk, stood, and stretched, relieved to have emerged from the dense growth of trees. He began looking at the view, continuing to turn his head until he'd seen the full one-hundred-eighty degree panorama of ocean stretched before him. A flock of pelicans propelled themselves across the sky like a flying necklace, and the Cove seemed remote from here, a safe haven from the jagged outcroppings being bashed directly below him.

He stepped out onto a ledge and began inching his way down the steep climb, still looking for Miranda. Finally he saw her, sitting with her arms wrapped around her knees, far below, on the tiniest beach he'd ever seen. At high tide there'd be no beach at all, but her timing was good, and what little sand existed was dry for the moment.

She seemed so self-contained and serene, hugging her solitude to her in a comfortable gesture. Yet there was something defenseless about her too, an unstudied vulnerability, which read like an invitation he knew he'd already accepted.

He made the climb down to her and extended his hand. The gesture came naturally, instinctively. She looked up at him, her eyes searching his, both asking for and supplying the answer. Their eyes still held as Miranda gave him her hand and he pulled her up easily, lifting her off the sand and into his arms. They stood on their private beach, embraced by wind, sheltered by rock. It was a beginning.

Chapter 9

Zelda McIntyre had worked hard since morning without taking a lunch break, and her thoughts were beginning to stray toward food. She'd been in a deliciously investigative mood all afternoon. The conversation with Miranda had been a tidbit to whet her appetite. Now she wanted to see if she could find any more tender morsels. It was a failing, she sometimes admitted to herself—her hunger for gossip. But then again, she turned whatever she found to splendid advantage with her ability to mix unusual ingredients.

"Zackery Calvin," she rolled the name around her tongue. From Santa Barbara. It sounded familiar. *Of course,* she almost said out loud. *That has to be Joseph Calvin's son, of Calvin Oil.*

Zelda considered this for a moment. She looked down at her hands, making a mental note to redo her polish that night and shorten her nails. Polished nails were professional; long ones were obscene.

I'll have to do a little digging and see if she's done it again, she mused. Miranda had a maddening ability for stumbling across the right people. Maybe it wasn't really stumbling, Zelda reluctantly considered, but was in the genes. On the other hand, one could put it down to excellent training. Zelda decided the latter was a more plausible theory. She was a great believer in upbringing and training, perhaps because she herself had had to earn both.

She picked up her Cross pen and wrote the name *Joseph Calvin* in a beautifully fluid hand. She considered the parties or events such a man might logically attend. She was wasting time. Stacked heels hitting the polished parquet floor, she flipped open her appointment book to check her late afternoon schedule.

Z elda's heels connected with the marble and sank into the plush carpeting by turns as she traversed the geometric design of the upper floor foyer of Calvin Oil. She was courteous but aloof with the elderly secretary who stood to greet her outside the CEO's office, turning on the charm when the boss emerged.

"Ah, Ms. McIntyre, how nice to meet you."
Dashing—there was no other way to describe him: the hair steel gray, the face clean shaven, the handshake firm. "The pleasure is mine, Mr. Calvin. It's very good of you to see me, especially on such short notice."

He ushered her in.

Flawless, she thought. *Classic Art Deco: circa 1915 leaded-glass doors, 1930 sideboard with the Eugene Printz signature folding doors and a newly-constructed desk to match, which makes even the fax machine look stylish.* "My, this is a stunning office. Art Deco is one of my favorite periods."

"We like to work in a pleasant environment." Joseph motioned her to be seated and walked around behind his desk. "I understand you've met my son Zackery." His voice was smooth and rich.

"Is that what your secretary told you? I'm sorry, actually

it was an artist I represent who met Zackery."

Joseph knew his secretary's patterns after all these years. Mary wouldn't make a mistake like that. So Zelda had more than one agenda at this meeting. Joseph's eye followed the fold of her wrap dress, the two sides of which didn't overlap until they met at her alligator belt.

Good, she thought. *A man with an eye. I was right not to wear the suit.* The late afternoon light glinted off her Cartier brooch and shadowed her contours in golden-red light. With any luck, that flattering glow would hold just until their meeting concluded. Then the sun would slip below the horizon, and she'd find herself having an unexpected dinner date. Zelda slid the Hermes scarf away from her throat, and made sure there wasn't too much of a business edge to her voice. "She indicated he was very interested in her work."

"I see." Joseph missed no details as he lifted his gaze to her face and sat in his plush office chair. "Did I understand she paints natural subjects—wildlife and outdoor scenes?"

"That is her specialty, and she does her work to perfection." Zelda bent forward to reach for her portfolio. The dress gaped enough to give Joseph a better view of her ample chest. "Of course, I can't say much for her personal politics, but that doesn't really come into it, does it? The artistic temperament is the price we must pay for art." She laughed pleasantly.

Joseph did not share the laugh. "I would have thought it was the artist who had to pay the price, rather than us, Ms. McIntyre."

Embarrassed at her gaffe, Zelda moved quickly to the next subject. "Oh, well, of course you're quite right." *A sensitive man*, she registered, *with a social conscience..unusual in a corporate decision-maker*. "Mr. Calvin, as divinely tasteful as your offices are, don't you feel there's something missing?"

Keeping a steady gaze on her, he replied, "I'm sure you'll

tell me if so, Ms. McIntyre."

Her chin jutting forward defensively, she made her reply a smooth one. "Works of art, Mr. Calvin. You could enhance this room with, well—depending upon your taste—anything from Picasso to Tamara de Lampika."

He shot back, "I don't think nudes quite fit the corporate image, do you Ms. McIntyre?"

She smiled, and it partially covered the blush creeping up her neck. Her remark had been calculated to test both his wallet and his breadth of knowledge, and she'd half expected his artistic expertise. But the fleeting mention of a nude had flashed like heat lightning, and now the atmosphere was charged, heavy with the promise of a storm.

"I see you're extremely well-informed." She collected herself before continuing. "I've been giving some thought to your needs as an oil corporation, and it occurs to me that your public image would be greatly enhanced by environmental works of art, wouldn't you agree?"

Drawing a hand across his chin, he thought about her remark. "I do agree with you there."

Zelda opened the portfolio on her lap. "I took the liberty of bringing some reproductions with me. You see this is one of Ms. Jones's recent pieces, now hanging in the Finders' Gallery in Milford-Haven." She lifted the burgundy leather portfolio across the desk to him, then leaned in.

He looked down and never took his eyes off the fold in her dress as he stood. He began to reach across the desk, hesitating only slightly. *Is he really the kind of man who'd make his first move by grabbing my breast?* Zelda met his gaze steadily, determined not to flinch if this was his tactic. He wouldn't be the first CEO to be brazen behind corporate doors.

He reached instead for the half-glasses he kept folded

upright in a leather holder directly in front of her. His gaze still held as he looked over the top of the glasses into her cleavage, rising and falling with her breathing. He lifted the portfolio, angling the page to avoid the late afternoon glare. His eyes swept across the printed landscape, then returned to her. "That's a stunning piece." He replaced his glasses.

"I'm glad you think so." *Have I been rebuffed, or is he still gathering his nerve? This is no time to retreat.* "What would you say to allowing me to look around for you, and bring one or two more samples for you to see?" Innuendo hung heavily in the dying sunlight.

Joseph considered her for a moment longer. He'd grown physically uncomfortable and needed to adjust himself. The arousal annoyed him; he wasn't sure why. "I'd be pleased if you'd do that Ms. McIntyre." He snapped the portfolio shut, a signal of closure.

Zelda pushed herself away from his desk. "I'm sure you won't be disappointed, Mr. Calvin." She turned, grasping the edge of her scarf and sliding it off the heavy vintage chair. She draped it expertly into the fold of her dress---her own signal of closure. She picked up the portfolio, then extended her hand. "Many thanks for our meeting. I'll be calling you soon."

That was usually his line. "You're...welcome." Joseph found he could not move from behind the desk. "My secretary will show you out."

Zelda withdrew her hand, then finally broke eye contact with the man, exiting quickly. She was miffed, and damn well not going to let him know it. *How dare he look at me that way, then dismiss me! I've brought harassment suits for less!* Her heels hitting the marble, she pressed the down button, and yanked her scarf out of her cleavage, suddenly hot.

The wait was interminable. She forced herself into professional mode. By the time the elevator doors opened, she'd already made her preliminary choices of what to bring to Joseph Calvin, and in which rooms they should hang. She'd also made a mental note not to let Little Miss Environment know that her paintings would soon grace the walls of an oil company. The ideas filed themselves with practiced discipline into their appropriate categories, to be remembered in perfect detail when she needed them. Joseph Calvin, CEO, slid comfortably into the client list, and she closed the mental file.

She welcomed the closing of the elevator doors, yet as she descended, her thoughts kept returning to the floor above. He'd played his cards close to his vest, and been blatant all at the same time. Or had all the blatancy been on her side? She'd asked for the meeting. He'd had the home court advantage. She'd brought a professional presentation. But he'd looked at her *that way*. Then she'd offered herself. And he'd rejected her. That was the bottom line.

She wanted retaliation. But not the usual kind. This time she wanted a revenge sweeter than *crème brûlé* and twice as smooth. She would have that dinner date soon, she thought. And with one corner of her Hermes scarf, she soaked up the tiny beads of sweat that had collected between her breasts.

As she left, Joseph felt a certain relief. Zelda McIntyre was not the kind of person one could be comfortable with. She created tension.

She also created a vivid impression; he'd give her that. He liked that in a woman. It's what had drawn him to Chris Christian. But for all her honesty and directness, Chris had subtlety. McIntyre was obvious. Perhaps it came with being voluptuous. That chest was heroic, and she knew exactly what to do with it. He found himself drifting into arousal again. It was unsettling.

He felt disloyal. He and Chris had an understanding. Neither of them wanted commitment, and there were few expectations. He knew she saw other men. He did his best to ignore that fact, and allowed himself, instead, to imagine that all her late dates were business appointments. Against his better judgment, he found that he cared for her increasingly.

He thought back to two mornings ago. They were both early risers, by habit perhaps more than by choice. They'd spent the night at her place this time, and he'd been lying by her side, enjoying her quiet breathing and the first rays of light filtering through slatted blinds, landing softly on her blond hair. A wave of tenderness swept over him then, a combination of protectiveness and desire. She'd looked so young. "Not that young!" she'd often chastise him. "What's a fifteen-year age difference between friends? I'm thirty five going on sixty," she'd say. She was right, as usual, wise beyond her years.

In that quiet moment he'd stroked her hair and it wakened her. The usually wise and wily eyes opened into a vulnerable and willing soul mate, and they clung to each other with a passion as deep as need. If it was love, they weren't ready to admit it.

And then her phone rang. She reached for it automatically, but he was on top, and from there it was easy for him to press her arms back into the bed. It turned into a rousing arm- wrestling session while her machine broadcast her message. *"You've almost reached Chris Christian with Satellite News, and if I'm not here, I'm covering a story. After the beep, you know what to do."*

They missed the last sentence. "Time for some real coverage, Calvin," she giggled, using her *aikido* expertise to roll over on him, pinning him down in turn.

"How do you do that? Show me those muscles," he teased.

"How many times do I have to tell you...it's not about muscles, Calvin."

She was the only woman who'd ever called him by his last name. Then that other voice issued forth from the box, constrained by the small speaker, but nonetheless menacing. Her mood changed immediately, though he tried to ignore it at first. *"Ms. Christian, you know who this is."* He couldn't remember exactly what the man had said. Something about the time frame changing. If she wanted the story, she now had only twenty-four hours to get it.

He tried to recapture their playful moment, but the message had brought Chris to full alert. He felt petulant, deserted. "Do you always get such mysterious messages?" he demanded. Even when it was a business call, he felt jealousy creeping into the room.

"Always" she teased, and in one fluid motion, slid off him and exited to the bathroom. "Are you pouting?" she called from the shower. "Don't pout, Calvin."

"We're still on for tonight, right?" he answered.

Her reply was a silky piece of underwear flung into the room. It landed on his head, and he laughed in spite of himself.

"Count on it," she said as she sashayed past and snatched the underwear.

He'd waited for her to join him for dinner that night. He'd had James prepare something simple at the house. She'd said not to wait past 11 p.m., that if things got that late, she'd go straight home and call him the next day. She did sometimes forget to call. She did sometimes get called out of town on a story. She'd been known to call from some airport, dashing between planes. But their dinner date had been for two nights ago.

Now he was beginning to worry.

Chapter 10

Samantha Hugo's living room was a reverie of Art Nouveau. Perhaps unconsciously, every line mirrored her own stately curves. Tall, long and curvaceous, she chose like-shaped objects. The graceful clock with pewter embellishments was perhaps more like Samantha than any other single piece she owned. It performed its function perfectly, and looked beautiful doing so.

Her own coloring resonated through her home as well—burnt orange and soft brown, ochre and dark chocolate. Having indulged her passion for flowers, a vibrant autumn arrangement seemed to pulsate on her coffee table—orange lilies and bright yellow sunflowers with their dark brown centers, deep burgundy dahlias, red Hypericum berries and coral zinnias.

The early morning light was less forgiving in the kitchen, where the answering machine was wedged among three months of letters, two weeks of newspapers, a year and a half of correspondence, and a collage of sticky-notes. The built-in table designed for informal dining had been usurped, and the tall kitchen stool served as the office chair. This was the heartbeat of the house, the rest all elegantly appointed appendages. It came as a package, the elegance with the efficiency, the order with the chaos.

When the phone rang, Samantha was in her bathroom doing a careful but quick job with an eyeliner pencil. She was torn between allowing another stoppage in an already badly interrupted morning, and letting the machine add to the omnipresent list of calls to be returned. Her machine picked up.

"Hello, this is Samantha Hugo. I'm sorry I can't come to the phone now. Please leave a message, and I'll get back to you as soon as possible." She only wished that were true.

Before the machine could quite complete its beep, her secretary was already talking. Today there was an edge to her voice, and perhaps just a twinge more than the usual annoyance.

"___antha, this is Susan at the office. I thought you said you'd be here by nine. In any case you have an urgent letter—it just arrived. You better get down here right away and see what it is."

Susan Winslow was thrilled to be at work early. Just as she was thrilled that her hangover was causing her head to throb. In fact, she was altogether thrilled to be awake on planet Earth today, and most particularly thrilled to be hunched over a filing cabinet. Her leather jacket made her feel hot, but as it was the only good thing about this day, she opted to keep it on.

The topic of her filing efforts was another thrill—oil spills. She tried to decide where the report on the latest disaster in Wales should be filed. "Oil: spills" seemed logical. But other files were labeled, "Oil: coastal" and "Oil: Wales."

Samantha's rubber-soled shoes made no sound as she entered the Environmental Planning Commission. A little out of breath, she said, "I got here as soon as I could."

Startled by the sound of Samantha's voice, Susan pulled up too quickly, banging her head on the edge of the file cabinet. "Shit," she said.

"Good morning to you too, Susan. Where's that letter?"

"Thanks for all the sympathy. It's right here. Who's it from?"

Samantha stood looking at her assistant, her face implacable. "Really, Susan, you ask rather personal questions."

"Do I?"

Samantha leaned over her desk. "I'm sure you've already looked for yourself."

"I was just, like, curious."

"I'll be in my office." Samantha closed her door. Susan's overactive curiosity was both an asset and a liability. Her skills in keeping the office running smoothly were considerable, but her insolent attitude sometimes pushed Samantha to the edge of tolerance.

Now that the physical door was closed, Samantha closed the mental one as well. Running her finger over the return address, she wasn't surprised to see it was from Associated Adoption Agencies. Ambivalent about what the contents would reveal, she paused before opening it. In the next moment curiosity won out over anxiety, and she tore open the envelope.

"Dear Ms. Hugo," it began. "We are in receipt of your request...." Her eye skipped over the boilerplate language and landed on the first pertinent bit of hard information. She hardly realized she was reading aloud. "Unfortunately, most of our records were destroyed in a fire several years ago."

She flung the letter onto her desk and strode through her door, opening it suddenly enough to see Susan make a quick adjustment. Although her sharp eye missed nothing, she found Susan irrelevant at the moment. She pulled a small plastic water bottle from the office refrigerator and was back in her office with the door reclosed before Susan had a chance to formulate an excuse.

Samantha took a long pull on the cold water and then picked up the letter again. "From the remaining files, we have been able to ascertain that your son was probably adopted within the state of California. We regret that we do not have an actual name or address to which we can refer you."

It was almost worse than hearing nothing, she decided, this limbo of knowing and not knowing. She picked up her water and tried to take a sip. When, instead, it spilled down her chin, she put it down disgusted, and stood looking out her office window. Gregory. She wondered if that was still his name. Probably not. They'd have given him a name they liked, even if they did find the embroidery—or perhaps especially if they found it.

Before she could stop it, she found herself engulfed in the rush of sights and sounds that had played so often in her head—the upturned face, the size-one shoes, the firm grasp of her finger, the first word, the trips to the Cove. How he used to love that cove. Bitterly, she realized he'd remember none of this, that somewhere there was a man who'd once been her son, and that she didn't even know his name.

Chapter 11

S ally rounded the edge of her counter just in time to see Deputy Johnson take a seat. She knew he'd want coffee for starters, so without pausing, she grabbed an upside-down mug from the just-washed shelf, slung it right-side-up and filled it with a deep splash from the freshly brewed pot she was carrying.

"Hey there Dep'ty, how's it flyin'?"

Delmar Johnson couldn't keep from smiling when he heard Sally O'Mally talk. He wasn't sure what it was. He never knew what Sally was going to say, but he knew it would always be original.

He was city born and bred, a native Angelino who'd served his time in South Central. Now he roamed the highways of the Central Coast, catching glimpses of the small-town life he'd never known. Human nature, he'd found, was essentially the same no matter the skin color or the location. People could always surprise him, whether for good or for ill.

His once-narrow world, though, had become wider, and his monochromatic palette was now a more colorful spectrum. It was the people he now met who provided this window for him, and he was as much a prism for them as they were for him. He and Sally would never have known each other had they not both gravitated to Milford-Haven. Prejudice stood like a well-tended wall between races in Arkansas, and fear acted like an electrified fence in L.A., segmenting neighborhoods as surely as if they were in different time zones. Now the unlikely pair had become friends.

"Not so good, huh? Don't tell me you're gettin' ready to skip one of my fabulous, gooey sticky cinnamon buns." That was the other thing. How was it she could read people so well? She was good. He'd have to ask for lessons.

"No cinnamon bun today, Sally."

"I know." *Ahhh noou*, it sounded like. "You just take your time. I'll be back before you can spin ten times on that stool." She was walking away, smiling, before he could say another word.

Samantha walked in and found a table without assistance, and was in no mood for the proprietress today. This had never stopped Sally before, and as she approached the table humming the inane tuneless string of notes that was her constant companion, Samantha was sure it wouldn't stop her today either.

"All alone today, Samantha? You know Jack is gonna be free for lunch.

Neither her tone nor her expression gave her away, yet there it was, Sally's opening salvo. *How do Southern women do that,* wondered Samantha. *How do they .mask their intentions so well?* It was a technique she both disrespected and envied at this moment.

"That won't be necessary Sally," Sam countered. "Do you think you can find time to bring me a cup of coffee?"

"Coffee's bad for you, Samantha, especially on a day like today." Sally's face was implacable, as before.

Samantha raised her voice in spite of herself. "What is *that* supposed to mean?"

"Well, do your hands always shake like that?"

If Miranda hadn't arrived at that moment, Samantha would've walked out of Sally's Restaurant. As it was, her effort to stand succeeded only in knocking over her water glass. All three women grabbed for the glass, but its contents hit the front of Samantha's blouse before they could stop it.

"See what I mean? I told you you were nervous. I'll be right back and clean that up for you. It's only water so it won't hurt nothin'." While Sally ran for the kitchen, Miranda grabbed napkins from the next table and went to work on Samantha's chair. Sally returned with a wad of paper and aimed at Samantha's chest, which met Sally at eye level. "Of course, on that print nothin' would show anyway." Sally's prattle seemed only to compound the error.

Samantha did her best to fend her off. "I can clean it up myself," she muttered between clenched teeth as she grasped the paper towels and began stabbing at the front of her soaked blouse.

The scene was comical, but in deference to her friend's feelings, Miranda refrained from laughing. "Sally, why don't you bring us a couple of coffees?" It seemed the best way to rescue these two opponents from a further altercation.

"What *is* it with her?" Samantha demanded, reluctantly giving up the battle with her blouse.

Ignoring the question, Miranda changed the subject. "I got your call. What's going on?"

The question helped Samantha stop spinning in frustration. "I got something in the mail," she answered bluntly.

"Gee, I wish I would get something in the mail." Sally was back with the coffee. "Here you go, girls. Anythin' else?"

"That's it, Sally." Miranda felt awkward in her self-appointed role of diplomat, dismissing Sally in order to keep the peace with Sam. And yet Sam needed her, and she could only hope that Sally would understand.

"So what was in the mail?" she asked. Whan Samantha

remained silent, Miranda continued. "It's about the adoption agency, isn't it?" Samantha's nod was enough of an answer. "Did they give you the name of the people who adopted him?"

"No. They don't have it. Their records were destroyed."

It was like sitting on a train, and being told it wouldn't be going any farther. Samantha jabbed at a tear collecting in the corner of her eye. The two friends sipped their coffees quietly. "Don't they know anything about where he might be?" Miranda asked after a while.

"Chances are he remained here in California," she said. "California's a big place."

"That does narrow it down a little." Miranda hated to sound like the eternal optimist. "What if you placed an ad...something that could run in some California magazine?"

"How am I going to run an ad when I don't even know his name!" Samantha protested.

"No, no, you could advertise to find one of those family search organizations, the ones who track down adopted children."

"You mean instead of combing through the yellow pages for every city in California, run an ad which says 'derelict Mother seeks abandoned child, needs help' ?"

Somehow the sarcastic humor cut through their morose mood, and the two friends found themselves laughing. Talking to Miranda had eased enough of Sam's tension that she felt she might be able to get back to work. Now there was a place to start. She wasn't giving up on finding her son. She was just getting started.

S ally didn't know exactly what it was, but there was something in the wind. She'd seen Samantha in a bad mood before, but not like this. And all right, so Miranda was Samantha's friend. But Miranda was her own friend too. The awkwardness when Sally had stood at their table had been thick enough to spread on toast. *Shoot,* thought Sally, *I never did get close enough to hear exactly what they were saying. Meanwhile, here I am stargazing in the daylight, and ignoring customers.* She made her way back to Del at the counter.

"So, Dep'ty, what'll it be?" She wet her pencil and held it poised over her order booklet.

"Why so formal?"

"Well, you didn't come in to eat today, so you must be here on biz'ness."

"You're too fast for me, Sally." He gave her a sidelong glance, ran his hand over his head, and pursed his lips. "Okay," he said. "I need you to look at something." He reached into the large, flat manila envelope he'd carried in with him. "Do you recognize her?"

"Well, 'course I do. She's that one from Satellite News. Oh, yes, I know that face. Couldn't tell you her name though."

"Christiana Christian."

"Well, moon in the mornin'." There was one of Sally's expressions again. This time Delmar didn't smile.

"What...you know her?"

"That's the name he gave."

Delmar could feel his skin begin to prickle. "The name who gave?"

"Well, I don't know. Never had seen him before."

Delmar's mind was racing, and he forced it into the deliberate slowness he had trained himself to use for investigations. "Back up a minute. There was a man—but you don't know who—and he knew Ms. Christian?"

"All's I know is, this man sat right here at my counter, and he was all nervous like, and when I asked him who he was waitin' for, he gave her name. Didn't ring a bell then. But I never can keep names in my head. Faces, though, well they stay clear as the view out my Mama's picture window."

As Sally described the man sitting at the counter, Delmar lifted his hands as though he might be able to salvage fingerprints. He was too late by hours, the way Sally ran a rag over every surface. He was afraid he was too late for Christiana Christian too.

"How did you know he was waiting for someone?"

Sally cocked her head and put a hand on a hip. "Oh, I just knew. You get to readin' customers after a time."

"Sally, would you be willing to come down to the Sheriff's station and work with one of our sketch artists?" Sally made a face—a new one, and one that put a smile back on Delmar's, in spite of himself. "You might be helping us a lot."

"All the way over to San Luis? I got to get back to my stew! And I hardly got to looking at that man's face at all. I was too busy with customers."

"Couple of hours," he countered.

She made another face.

"All right, I'll have you outta there in one hour."

"Well, I'll think about your sketchin' man, Delmar. But I got one real important errand to do first."

He was relieved to have her call him by his first name again. It meant they were still friends. Friends did favors. And Delmar needed one.

It was a five-minute walk to Sawyer Construction on a slow day, and today Sally covered the distance in three. She found no one in the outer office, and thought that was just as well, as she was in no mood to be interrupted. "Jack! Jack are you in there?" she called as she knocked on the door to his private office. "Jack! I know you're in there, and I have to see you right now!"

Jack Sawyer had remained as silent as possible during Sally's door-pounding. It was one thing to see her privately, but this intrusion into his workplace was unwelcome. Obviously, she wasn't going away. "All right, Sally, but I'm in the middle of a million things. Make it snappy." He barely glanced at her as he opened his door and returned to his chair. It creaked as he sat down, and he made no attempt to offer seating to his guest.

Sally was positively gleeful, and it made her even more annoying than usual. "I have some information for you," she sang.

"Well? What is it?" he barked the words, trying to hurry this along.

"It's *private* information."

"It's always private information with you, Sally, and it never amounts to anything. So get it out and get it over with."

If Sally heard either his words or his tone, she paid attention to neither. "Well, I think first of all I'll just make myself at home right over here." She pulled a rickety chair away from the wall and watched with a grimace as its legs left tracks in the floor's accumulated dust. "You ought to clean this place more than once a year, Jack." Sally sat, and pulled off her shoes as she spoke, allowing them to fall noisily to the floor. "You know, a girl like me spends so many hours on her feet, you just wouldn't believe how awful tired she can get."

This whole encounter was trying Jack's patience, but he knew if he tried to hurry her any further he would only succeed in slowing her down. "Fine, Sally," he said deliberately, "take a load off your feet, but remember I haven't got all day for this."

"Oh, you know this morning when I was makin' up my first batch of biscuits, I was thinkin' an awful lot about that time we went over to the big Central Coast Fair."

Jack chewed the edge of his lip and stared out through his spatter-encrusted window. Now she was apparently getting romantic. "I told you, Sally, I don't have all day."

"And how you told me none of those other ladies could cook a lick compared to me, and my biscuits won the prize that day and all."

How long he could listen to this he wasn't sure. "Yes, yes, that was all very nice, Sally, but can you please get to the point? I've got men waiting at a construction site."

Undeterred, she droned on. "Well, anyway, I was just thinking about what a nice time that was, and how I liked tellin' you things about myself after that, 'cause I felt like I could trust you, and then..."

If she was fishing for compliments, her timing was off. He thought about how carefully he kept his temper in check when he spoke with customers in his office—then remembered she wasn't one. "Look, Sally, I'm simply gonna have to leave. I can call you later at the restaurant, or you can call me, but right now I've got a meeting and people are waiting for me."

Jack stood to go, relieved that he would finally escape this meaningless interview. He was surprised at Sally. She was usually clever enough to attempt these relationship discussions when she'd pumped him full of her excellent cooking, or had him where she wanted him in bed.

Sally jumped up from her chair and moved fast, intercepting him. She placed a tiny hand on his barrel chest, but it was her tone of voice that stopped him. "I told you I had private information for you, Jack. And I think this is somethin' you are gonna want to hear from *me* instead of from someone else."

Neither the tone nor the gesture did anything for his temper, which was near its boiling point. "What kind of information, Sally?"

"It's about a child, Jack."

The sentence hit him like a two by four. "What? Do you mean to tell me you're...?"

Jack stood suspended in an agony of anxiety, and she gave him no relief. "I'm not tellin' you nothin', Jack, until you sign this." She slapped a piece of paper down on Jack's desk.

She was all calm and coolness as she collected her shoes, replaced the chair legs in their original spots, and opened his door to leave. "Y'all have a nice day," she said.

It was his least favorite expression.

Chapter 12

Zack was enjoying his aimlessness immensely. The afternoon sun filtered through the tall pines and seemed to strike the café's outdoor tables at long, lazy angles. The specialty of the house was freshly brewed raspberry iced tea, and it was delicious enough to tempt the hummingbirds out of the trees, but with the pleasant chill in the air, he opted for a pot of hot Orange Pekoe. There were plenty of outdoor cafes back in Santa Barbara, but there was nothing like the peace of this place.

He'd explored Main Street from one end to the other, then walked to the end of the pier, finding Michael's Restaurant, Milford-Haven's only foray into gourmet fare. The place was closed for the afternoon, but its kitchen doors were open. Enticed by the aromas, Zack stepped inside and found Michael himself preparing the evening's offerings. The ensuing conversation between the two men revealed a shared passion for fine food and a lively debate over California versus France in all things culinary. Before leaving, Zack booked a table for tonight's date with Miranda.

She'd agreed to see him again, sharing his last night in town. He felt only slightly guilty that he'd disrupted her schedule in the last couple of days. Her life was ordered and disciplined—she obviously got an enormous amount of work done. And yet her life had a spontaneity his lacked.

Life seemed to happen to her. His life in Santa Barbara was a structured agenda neatly entered into his personal info system. Mary input his appointments. James picked up his pressed shirts. All this was supposed to leave him free for his higher purpose. But lately he'd felt neither free nor purposeful.

He'd enjoyed the work in his twenties. Being the youngest member of his Harvard Business School graduating class to make Vice President was no mean achievement, even if it *was* the family firm. Fellow students knew such a volume of dollars and decisions required focus and stamina. He had plenty of both.

He'd also enjoyed Dad. Over the years they'd forged a bond few men seemed able to create. In fact, they were living the classic dream. Father and son, CEO and VP, united in business and work ethic, competitive in sport, gentlemanly with women. The two most eligible bachelors in Santa Barbara, one for each age bracket. They saw each other at work, kept their distance after hours unless they attended the same social function. Occasionally they entertained together.

Lately, though, Zack had begun to have the constant feeling he was repeating himself. It was a sensation he tried to outrun, and with his schedule it'd been easy for a while. More ambitious quarterly goals. More international partnerships. More meetings. More squash matches. More yacht parties. And more evenings with Cynthia.

Suddenly disturbed at the thought of Cynthia, he and remembered he hadn't called her all weekend. He hadn't called anyone. In fact, he hadn't even checked his messages. He glanced at his watch. Dad might need him for something. Zack pulled his checkbook-thin cell phone from his breast pocket. Reluctantly, he dialed his own number to check for messages..

"Zackery, darling... it's me." There it was, that throaty voice. *"I miss you so much. Wait till you see what I'm almost wearing for Halloween. When are you coming back from that dreary little place up the road? What's it called? Mill Pond? You must be SO bored. Don't worry. Cynthia fix."*

There were no other messages. He collapsed his phone and terminated the call. Her message sent an arc of electricity traveling from one end of his synapses to the other, but left him feeling spent, as though the sudden charge had drained his battery.

The old, familiar malaise washed over him, his system overloading with conflicting data, slowing his response time and choking off his new-found contentedness. He could see Cynthia placing the call, twisting the phone cord around a long, manicured finger. She'd be reclining against her satin pillows, pouting petulantly as she waited for him.

That world seemed a dark one from this perspective, appealing to a shadow self which, for today, was banished by the gentle sun of this touching little town. How wrong Cynthia was, that he would be bored. How typical that she didn't recall the name of Milford-Haven, that she discounted it as some sort of backwater, unworthy of her ambitions, and, therefore, of his. How strangely relieved he was by the lack of obligatory socializing. And how satisfied he felt that he'd discovered a place of his own, something she knew nothing about, something he did not have to share.

It didn't occur to him to return the call. Her message had been intrusion enough into his remaining hours of freedom. He looked at his watch. Three hours until he would pick up Miranda for dinner. He suddenly thought of the Cove. A magical place. The thought of a long walk appealed to him. He would just have time before returning to his motel for a shower.

Zack looked around the Rosencrantz Garden Café one more time, left a generous tip on his table, and walked through the double doors, waving at his waitress as he left. He pressed the keyless entry device from across the parking lot, climbed into his Mercedes, and began driving toward the Cove.

Z elda's plans for sweet revenge were being formulated with meticulous care. She'd started with a full afternoon at the UCSB library, reading every microfiche on the busy corporate life of Joseph Calvin, tracking his astounding rise through the ranks of fellow Harvard grads, through the formation of Calvin Oil, and following his rapid-fire series of acquisitions.

Standard & Poors had been useful, *Value Line* even more so, with its comprehensive updates. The *L.A. Times* had done its share of covering Calvin Oil—particularly the Santa Barbara oil spill, which had generated plenty of ink at the time, and made the company infamous in Southern California. But of more interest were the *Wall Street Journal* piece—the front page column chronicling Joseph and his rise to power; and *The Financial Times,* which did the best job of tracking the flux and flow of quarterly earnings. She'd found it surprising that the British press had paid such attention to a relatively small U.S. oil firm, until they'd punctuated their coverage with details of the acquisition of West Wales Petroleum. It had not by any means been Joseph's first foray into the international arena. But it had been his son Zackery's. No doubt Joseph had watched the development of that deal like a hawk.

Zelda had also pored over the social pages of the *Santa Barbara Register*, carefully noting the name—and if possible the face and the wardrobe—of every woman seen on Joseph Calvin's arm over the past five years. Mostly they were thin, wispy things, she decided, WASPish and pearled, well-heeled and -coifed perhaps, but insubstantial in any decidedly womanly ways. Once or twice there seemed to be someone substantive—a female CEO or Ambassador—but they were always jowly and thick through the middle, vastly intelligent in conversation, she imagined, but not flirtatious. And Joseph liked flirtation. This much she knew.

Her own looks were very much in her favor, she felt, and so was her figure. This made the wardrobe choices easier, and she rearranged her closet, placing the "Joseph items" in one section for instant access in any emergency. He was tall, so she could wear her higher heels, and this was good too, as they sculpted the leg and automatically added drama and sex appeal to any outfit. She reviewed her scarf selection briefly, and then decided it was time to return calls before the close of business hours.

Cynthia Radcliffe's was the first message—the voice sounding too sensuous and vapid for a professional call. Still, it was Zelda's policy to return all calls.

"Yes, this is Zelda McIntyre. You called to invite me to a Museum Benefit—how very nice of you." Zelda had no idea who this Cynthia person might be. All the more reason to be polite until she did.

"How very nice of you to call me back." The voice tried to match her own. "Will you be able to attend?"

Zelda was losing interest, but decided at least to glance at her book. "When is it exactly?"

Cynthia seemed to be fumbling with something, and Zelda's patience was waning. "If you can hang on one moment...I have all the information right here...it's on the twentieth at 5 p.m. And of course it's to be held at the Calvin Estate."

"I beg your pardon?" Zelda refocused quickly. She had to be certain she'd heard correctly.

"The Calvin Estate. It's on San Marcos Road. Are you familiar with it?" Cynthia oozed superiority, but Zelda's mind was racing and she failed to notice.

"Oh, yes, of course, the Calvin Estate. Let me just write this down in my book, San Marcos Road, 5 p.m."

On the other end of the line, it did not escape Cynthia's notice that the woman had suddenly taken an interest. This might be someone to cultivate, particularly if it meant she'd have another ally at the party. An artists' representative. It sounded substantial, and the more substantial friends she had, the better. Her problem now was one of minor logistics—namely, balancing newspapers, phone, invitations, and Pink Passion nail polish in the center of her disheveled bed.

"So, the Calvin Estate." Zelda continued. "What a lovely setting. You and the Calvins must be great friends."

"Oh, we've been friends for years!" *Zelda might be a friend of the family. Better be more accurate.* "Well, one year. Ever since I moved here. We've been close since the day we met. You know how it is." *Treat her like a girlfriend. Let her in on a secret.* "Perfect chemistry. You must have seen our pictures together at all the big parties this season."

"You mean you attend these parties with Mr. Calvin?"

"Yes, with Mr. Calvin, Jr. With Zackery, that is. We just go everywhere together. We're practically engaged." For a moment Cynthia thought she might have overstepped her bounds, but Zelda seemed to take the comment in stride.

"Well, congratulations. I'm sorry, I must have missed the announcement."

"Oh! It hasn't been announced yet, but I'm sure any day now it will be." Panic rose in her throat. *What if Zelda was Joseph's confidante? What if she mentions this to Joseph before Zack has a chance? Zack would be furious!*

Interrupting her anxiety attack, Zelda remarked, "It's our little secret then."

Too relieved, Cynthia responded, "That's right! Well, it's so nice to meet you, over the telephone at least, and to make a new friend!"

"Yes, isn't it."

"Um, Zelda...I hope you don't mind my calling you by your first name. You know while I have you on the phone, there is something I would love to ask your help with." Though Cynthia got no response, she continued. "I read that you're an artists' representative, and I desperately need a wonderful gift to present to Zackery at the party, and I mean, what do you get the man who has everything? And this is a museum benefit, so I really must give a painting or something. Well, so, you know art, don't you?"

"It's what I do."

"Well, how about finding something for me? Something really impressive."

"What a fascinating idea, Cynthia." Zelda's mind seemed to engage. "I may be able to locate something for you. You wouldn't by any chance favor some sort of wildlife art, would you?"

Cynthia reclined further into her pillows and tried to picture what a wildlife would look like. Something woolly and large and masculine, she imagined. She certainly understood something about Zackery's animal instincts, but she wasn't sure she wanted any such thing on display. "I'm not sure about that idea, Zelda."

"Some sort of outdoor nature scene then?"

"Mmm. Yes, that would do. As long as it's tasteful."

"Oh, my yes, I don't represent anything but the finest work."

"So, Zelda, how does this work?"

"Leave everything to me. I have the perfect painting for you. I'll make arrangements to have it shipped immediately. Come to my office in two days, and I'll show it to you. But trust me. It's perfect."

"Oh, now I'm getting excited. Two days." Cynthia scrambled for a pen. "I suppose I'd better get the address of your office."

"Five-five-five and one-half State Street. Be there at 9 a.m."

"Oh, Zelda, can we say 10 a.m.? I'm really not a morning person."

"No, I'm sorry, but it's going to be a terribly busy week. See you at nine. Ta ta."

Before Cynthia could make any further objection, Zelda hung up the phone and began to ruminate on the fascinating scenario unfolding in front of her. She was dialing another number before the handset had cooled. Nicole's unmistakable French accent pronounced the greeting.

"You 'ave reach the Finders' Gallery. We are locate on Main Street in Milford-'aven, et if you would like, please leave us uh message, we will call you back. Merci."

"Nicole, dear, it's Zelda. I've made a sale and arranged an exhibit all in one event. I'll have to ask you to ship the seashore painting off to Santa Barbara immediately. You know the one, 'The Cove,' catalogue number 129. Even if you've had interest in the piece, this supersedes. And don't mention this to Miranda, let me do that. It'll be our little surprise."

Chapter 13

How long it'd been since Miranda had a real date, she couldn't remember, and she wasn't sure she still had the knack of dressing in anything but jeans.

Rummaging for the third time through her closet, her hand found the green dress and she yanked it off its hanger. When she held it up to check herself in the full length mirror, her jeans showed beneath the hem and her T-shirt protruded down her arms. Frustrated, she pulled off her clothes and tried again. It seemed to work, so she flung the dress to the bed and stepped onto the cold tiles of her shower, waiting for the water to heat.

By half an hour later, she was searching for a pale lipstick she'd once had, and looking for her favorite flats. All seemed well till she looked at her hands. Working quickly with an emery board, she tried to even the closely clipped nails and scrape the paint specks away from the cuticles.

Satisfied she'd done all she could, she stopped for another appraisal in the mirror. The silk dress had been a birthday gift from her sister. It floated when she moved, and then settled easily to reveal hip bones and thigh muscles. Its dark green color set off her eyes, accented now with the barest hint of eye makeup. She'd swept her hair to one side and captured it in a silver barrette so it fell over one shoulder. Reaching for the earrings with the Celtic knot that matched the barrette, she put the hooks through her ears and watched as light played on the shining metal. All in all, it was as much effort at dressing as she'd made in months, and she enjoyed the feeling.

Racing up the stairs, she rummaged in her hall closet for a wrap of some kind and found her Welsh woolen—dark green with complex twists of cabling, it was pinched at the waist and decorated with pewter buttons. Realizing she'd forgotten her purse, she ran downstairs and reached high into her closet for the one she was looking for—a flat envelope of soft green suede that matched her flats. Checking to see it contained the basic necessities, she tossed in the lipstick and a small brush as she climbed back to the foyer, then went to her studio to retrieve a small sketch pad—something she never traveled without.

Through the long bank of windows, she saw the last blood-red bands of sunset hanging suspended like undiluted paint stuck to an unfinished canvas. Absorbed in a color reverie, she gauged how much red ochre and gold amber she would need to mix to capture that sky. The last color was the most intense on some days—like today...the intensity of her second day with Zack. The thought that it could intensify still more sent a thrill down her long legs through to the end of her toes. But such intensity, she worried, could burn out just as quickly as the rapidly sinking sun.

B y the time Zack put his hand in the small of Miranda's back to guide her to their table, Michael's Restaurant was humming. On each table, clear vials of oil supported small flames that illuminated vivid miniature pumpkins hanging from their vines. Plates of pasta spun by as the *maître d'* seated them. "Your waiter will be right with you," he said as he glided Miranda's chair into place. Aromas of sauces and seasonings wafted past their table as servers delivered fragrant, steaming dishes.

Zack watched as Miranda settled in her chair. This afternoon, she'd reclined in the bucket seat of his car as though it'd been sculpted for her, but she'd seemed uncomfortable. Maybe he could change that tonight.

The dress she wore was just right—sleek and elegant without being formal. *She'd look great in emeralds,* Zack thought, *if she'd ever consent to wearing serious jewelry.* She smiled at him and looked down shyly, fidgeted with something in her lap, then looked out the window at the view.

Following her gaze, he noticed how different the twilight looked here. The darkened water was inky black. The lights were few—just enough to mark the coastline, unrelieved by offshore rigs or tankers. It seemed a cozy and deliciously remote setting.

Zack's musings were interrupted by a visit to their table. "Well, you said the lady was a local beauty. You didn't tell me she was a heart-stopper." Michael was in his element, playing the gracious host. "I see now why you gave me the third degree about tonight's menu."

Zack removed his napkin from his lap and began to stand. Before he could push his chair back, Michael had a hand on his shoulder. "No, no please don't get up. Just introduce me to your beautiful friend."

Miranda blushed, and her eyes darted to Zack. She was chafing under all this attention. Her eyes pleaded with Zack to make it all go away. Despite Michael's invitation to remain seated, Zack stood. "Michael Sandoval, chef, Miranda Jones, artist." Sensing Miranda's discomfort, Zack kept it simple.

Michael clicked his heels together and bent over Miranda's hand as he kissed it. She pulled her hand back the instant Michael let it go. The gesture wasn't lost on Zack. "Well, we're looking forward to the meal, Michael. Thanks for stopping by the table." Miranda's unstudied elegance had Michael transfixed, but through the spell, he heard the slight edge in Zack's voice. Territory he understood, especially where a beautiful woman was concerned. "Those sand dabs *meunières* will be right out." He withdrew reluctantly, covering his exit with charm, and returning to his role as gregarious host at the next table.

Zack stood for a moment longer, looking down at Miranda who'd resumed staring out the window. She was a puzzle, this woman. Sure of herself. Yet suddenly shy—painfully so. He reseated himself, pulled his chair in, and leaned across the table. "Are you all right?"

His remark seemed to startle her. "Oh. Sorry. Yes. Of course. Fine." She made an attempt to smile. Zack searched for a way to ask without asking, what might be behind her discomfort.

"I was hoping you'd like this restaurant. We can go somewhere else if you'd prefer."

"Oh, no! Not at all. I've never eaten here. Never been here at night. The lights... they're beautiful."

"I'm surprised."

"Surprised?"

"That you've never been here."

"I didn't say that." Discomfort flashed across Miranda's face. She turned towards the window.

"Well, if you'd ever been here before, Michael would never have forgotten." Zack couldn't read Miranda's expression.

"Miranda I just meant that you made quite an impression on him. He doesn't seem so easily impressed." He reached across the table, placing his hand over hers. "You're a beautiful woman. Why shouldn't he be impressed?"

Miranda turned to face him, the candle bouncing light from her green silk and igniting tiny emeralds in her eyes. The discomfort seemed to vanish, and the touch of their hands propelled them both back to their moment at the Cove.

They were interrupted again, this time by the arrival of the entrées. Miranda raised an eyebrow. "I can't decide whether to be flattered or offended."

"Because I ordered for you? Well, why don't you decide after you taste the food?"

"That's a neat way off the hook."

"Pun intended?"

Scowling slightly, Miranda looked at her plate—flawless presentation, irresistible aromas. She took his suggestion and lifted a morsel of tender fish to her mouth. "Mmm, superb." Between bites she asked, "When did you have time to make a reservation? And how did you find Michael's?" There was mischief in her eyes and Zack smiled.

"Nicole told me about it."

"At the Gallery? I didn't know Nicole gave out dining suggestions."

"I wanted to do a little homework."

Miranda tried a bite of winter squash. "What else have you found out about my little town?"

He looked in her eyes. "That it seems to be full of unexpected treasures."

The waiter appeared as if on cue with a bottle of local wine—chosen by Michael to complement the meal—and uncorked the bottle expertly, pouring the first sip into Zack's glass. Zack took his time eyeing the color, inhaling the fragrance, swilling the mouthful. Pronouncing it excellent, he signaled the waiter to pour.

"Well, how about a toast?" Zack offered. "To...the Cove."

Miranda touched the stem of her wine glass and hesitated.

"Something wrong?" Zack asked.

"No...I, well, I don't drink."

"Oh...I'm sorry. I just assumed...." Zack looked awkwardly at his glass and put it down.

"Oh, but please," she protested, "I don't mind if other people do, especially an excellent wine chosen by the chef."

Zack persisted. "Have a sip at least, or you'll offend our host."

"All right. One sip."

Chinking his glass against hers, he toasted, "To the most gracious woman in Milford-Haven." He took a swallow. "Mmm.You're right, it is excellent. So, tell me about this, why you don't drink."

"I'll tell you some time."

An awkward silence descended. After another bite of food Zack asked, "Did you grow up near here?"

"Yes...and no. Northern California. Near San Francisco."

"A native Californian! Like me."

"Santa Barbara has always been home for you?" she asked.

"All my life. So you gave up the big city for an artist's colony. Was that the draw?"

"Your turn for a pun."

"Touché. Really, though. Was that it?"

Growing pensive, Miranda stared at the lights trailing away to the end of the pier. "I don't know. Sometimes I think it's the lighting." Her eyes focused on his. "Lighting has so much to do with the visual identity of a place. In Africa it's...or like cities...been to Paris?"

He nodded.

"Okay, think of Paris. Then think of New York. They have completely different lighting, don't you think?

"Lighting?" Zack's expression was amused, tolerant. "Paris?"

"It's just...painter stuff." She changed the subject. "Speaking of cities, when did you first start coming to Milford-Haven?"

Zack shook his head and tried to keep up. "Just the other day."

"But Santa Barbara is so close...I can't believe you haven't been up here before. Your job must keep you very busy."

"My job—yeah! You wouldn't believe how busy."

"Doing what?"

"Now wait a minute, we were talking about lighting. Only an artist would even think of it. What do you mean exactly?" Zack took another mouthful of his dinner.

Miranda looked out the window for a moment, then shifted back to Zack. "I can paint my ideas much better than I can explain them.... Let's see. Imagine a city on a bright, sunny day. Whenever there's bright sun, there are also shadows, so what you really see is a light/dark cityscape—buildings throw dark gray shadows across one another, sidewalks bounce light back so brightly they seem almost white."

"High contrast." Zack took another swallow of his wine.

"Yes, almost like a black and white photograph, with thousands of shadings of gray. Now imagine that same city on an overcast day." Miranda's voice grew more animated as she visualized what she described.

"Sounds monochromatic."

"No! Not at all! The more subtle lighting enables you to

see the true colors. A park bench which might have seemed dark gray turns out really to be dark green; the water in a fountain no longer looks black, it picks up the blue and green of sky and algae; the yellow of a table-umbrella is so bright it looks like a little spot of sunshine. Diffused lighting intensifies all the colors, you see? Makes them pop out, instead of getting diluted by so many lumens from the sun." Miranda's face itself seemed illuminated.

Zack smiled.

"What?" she smiled back. "I'm going on, aren't I?"

"I think it's great! But you might want to take a bite of your dinner."

"Oh!" She grinned and took a bite.

Zack watched Miranda's mouth pull against her fork. It was difficult, but he was making the effort to focus on the woman's accomplishments. Anything to take his mind off that mouth. "It's a gift, you know."

"What is?" she asked.

"To know what you love. To *do* what you love."

"What else is there?" Miranda wondered. And what struck Zack as extraordinary in her comment, was that she meant it.

Zack stood when Miranda excused herself, then sat to enjoy the pleasant buzz of the wine as it seemed to soften the edges of the distant lights. When she arrived back at their table, so did their final course, and he failed to notice she'd returned without her purse.

Dessert was a lemon mousse, and Zack watched as Miranda ate slowly, savoring the delicate flavor. In a moment his own plate was empty, and he pushed it back. *Someday I'll learn to eat slowly, but never as sensuously as she does,* he thought. To distract himself, he asked, "What about that whale painting in your studio—where did that image come from?"

"I *care* about whales," she answered between bites.

"A lot of people say they care about whales. I don't see them capturing the look in a whale's eye as the harpoon takes him."

Miranda hesitated. "I was out there with them."

"Out there...where? Whale watching?"

"Three thousand miles into the North Pacific. You know, no one really enforces the quotas set up by the International Whaling Commission. And of course, the conservatives think it's all a waste of time."

"Oh, really." Zack couldn't mask the edge that crept into his voice. "So you became a self-appointed police force?"

Emerald fire flashed into Miranda's eyes. "We only have one planet, Zack. All creatures deserve respect."

Zack laughed.

"I'm sorry you find it amusing."

"No! No, Miranda." He touched her hand across the table. "It's just that...I'm trying to imagine the elegant woman across from me standing on the deck of some ship, sketching whales in a gale-force wind. And it's easier to picture than I thought."

She shook her head, but didn't seem convinced.

"That's really why you paint them, isn't it?" He continued. "Because you respect them."

"That's why I paint every creature I'm lucky enough to see. That's why I paint nature scenes. If I can make people connect with something they see...well, like you connected with the Cove." Her chest heaved as she tried to calm down.

"The Cove? Why would you say I'm connected to the Cove?"

If he'd trampled on her nerve a moment ago, now she'd

stepped on his.

"I didn't mean to suggest—"

"That's not why I love your painting, Miranda," he said, cutting her off.

"It's just that when we went there yesterday, you said the Cove looked familiar...." Miranda twisted her napkin in her lap.

"Oh. Well, must have been some childhood memory."

"A childhood...but I thought you said you'd never been to—"

Zack cut her off again. "Actually I *have* been to Milford-Haven, but I was so young I hardly remember it." Awkwardness hung over the table like the sudden low fog that was overtaking the pier. "Is your wine okay? Oh, that's right, you don't drink." He poured himself another half glass.

"The food was delicious, Zack."

Her mother must have trained her well, he thought. *Change the subject. Pay a compliment.* Zack used his napkin to wipe his mouth and moved his chair back enough to cross his legs. "Glad you enjoyed it." His tone was flat.

"So your parents brought you up the coast when you were little?" She asked.

"My...parents, yeah." He uncrossed his legs, crossed them the other way. "Did you start painting when you were a child?"

"Yes, when I— " Miranda choked, and took a sip of water. "When I was a child." The choking escalated.

Zack sat across from her feeling helpless. He lifted his water glass, offering her some, then saw his stupidity. The woman was choking on water. Miranda continued to cough. Zack stood, crossed to her, and began patting her on the back. By now other patrons in the restaurant had noticed her difficulty, and a silence was beginning to fall.

Miranda looked up imploringly at Zack. "I'm okay,

really," she said, her voice weak. "Please."

Understanding her dislike of attention, Zack sat down. "Are you?" He wanted to protect her, he found. Wanted to sweep her up and get her out of here. "I didn't mean to.... Did I upset you?"

Miranda laughed weakly. "They say if you choke when you're trying to say something, it means you're having trouble saying it."

"Or it could just mean you choked. You didn't catch a fish bone, did you?"

"No. Nothing like that."

She looked at Zack and it was his turn to have something catch in his throat. Something about her vulnerability. Something about her beauty, and a certain willingness in her eyes. "Are you ready to go?" he asked.

"I thought you'd never ask," she replied, in a voice so quiet he was glad he'd been listening carefully.

Miranda kicked off her flats and lit a fire. Zack seated himself at one end of her large, comfortable sofa, and she took the opposite end, swinging her legs onto the middle cushion, until her toes were almost touching him.

Something about the way she sat there, hugging a pillow, hiding at the far end of the sofa struck him as endearingly childlike. And yet as the firelight struck the angles of her high cheekbones and glinted off the green silk covering the long, sleek curves of the legs stretched toward him, he knew she was all woman.

Zack kicked off his shoes and swung his legs up parallel to hers. She tucked his feet under the pillow she was holding. Invited thus far into intimacy, he responded by resting his arm on her shin, his hand cupping her knee. "Throat feel okay?" he asked. "No more choking?"

"No," she said. "I'm fine."

"So what was it?"

She hesitated as though trying to avoid his question, then answered, "It's just this business of being a painter that got stuck in my throat." Almost absent-mindedly, Miranda began to knead his toes.

Zack squinted and tried to concentrate on what she'd just said. "You're kidding. It's your passion. You're a natural." The kneading felt divine.

"That's not how my parents saw things." Miranda glanced over at the fire, and Zack saw tension in her jaw as she stared into the flames. She squeezed his foot harder now, finding knots he hadn't known were there.

"What, your parents didn't approve?" Miranda shook her head. "Not enough profit potential?" Miranda looked at him, said nothing and moved her strong hands to his other foot. "Not the right sort of activity for a young lady?"

"Very perceptive." Miranda blinked, looking as though a secret had been discovered.

"Well, you showed them," he said. He struggled to keep the conversation going, fighting his impulse to respond to her touch, afraid that if he did she'd withdraw and the moment would be shattered.

"I did?" Miranda wasn't being coy, he decided, her question was genuine. She worked his foot diligently, focused on her task.

He felt he'd have to respond now, or explode. He looked above the fireplace and found a means of escape by focusing on her painting of the Mara in Kenya—a panoramic view as clear and compelling as a window. "Any artist as successful...and as talented...as you are.... Well, you've got it all."

"Mmm." Miranda looked up at the painting, and seemed to lose herself in some faraway trip to Africa. The fire crackled and burned low. The woman's mind was far away. But her body was right here. Zack didn't need much reminding.

Moving his hand against her leg, he began massaging her thigh. As an involuntary murmur escaped her lips, he felt a surge of electricity pulse through him, propelling him forward. As he ran his hands up her long silk curves, Miranda's upturned face told him everything he needed to know.

Chapter 14

Early morning sunlight struck the wall of Susan's room, penetrating its thin layers of black paint like a spotlight through a cheap see-through slip.

Any rays of light that hadn't been absorbed by the black ricocheted and then hit her eyes like so many pellets. She groaned and pulled the black bed sheet over her face. The flesh around her new nose ring was still sore, and she cursed as the soiled linen dragged across the inflamed tissue. She lifted the sheet gingerly and tried to open her eyes.

The garish display of favorite rock-star posters on the wall opposite her bed seemed to leer at her, mocking her discontent like haughty creatures looking through from another dimension.

In that other dimension she'd be recognized, valued, understood. If the force of her thought could have propelled her through the wall and into the future, she'd have landed in 2020, the rock star of her age, adored by her fans, pursued by men, her every whim indulged.

As it was, she had only twenty minutes to get to work. She rolled across the thin mattress, cursing again at the inadequate cushioning it provided against the bare floor, and struggled to stand.

A minute later she was in the all-in-one fiberglass shower-tub, enduring but not enjoying the rush of warm water.

Why, she wondered, had he not agreed to take her with him? That guy she'd met at the bar and his band would've left at four this morning, and by now she'd have been on the road, and out of this black hole of a town. She'd escaped the impoverished Reservation down in the Santa Ynez Valley only to find herself stuck in a white man's nightmare.

And the white woman I work for is a heartless bitch. But that's okay, she thought. *She'll pay.* And with that, Susan smiled for the first time that morning.

Ten minutes later, Susan was dressed for the day. Her leather jacket squeaked reassuringly, and her micro-skirt rose to its last possible height as she sat on the edge of the mattress to use the phone. She lifted the receiver and hit the speed-dial button.

"Hello. You have reached Samantha Hugo at the Environmental Planning...."

"Bla bla bla," Susan talked back to the machine, allowing the message to play through while she fingered the ad torn from the *Milford-Haven News*. When she heard the familiar beep, she said, "Samantha, it's Susan. I was calling to say I'm late. I certainly thought *you'd* be in by now." She'd practiced her sarcastic tone to a fine point. "I think I've found somebody who can track down that important person you need to find. I'll tell you about it at the office later. Save a couple of private moments for me."

In the Environmental Planning Commission washroom, Susan stood in front of the mirror and inspected her nose. The new hole was still surrounded by slight inflammation, and as she tried to decide how worried to be, she rehearsed her speech.

"There's something I've been meaning to ask you, Samantha." *No way. Polite never gets you anywhere*, she thought.

"It's been seven months and three days, Samantha, and in view of the indispensable service I provide to you and the Environmental Planning Commission, I think it's appropriate to request an adjustment to my salary." *Oh puh-leeze. No way can I pull off the logic act,* she decided.

"What you pay me doesn't come close to compensating me for all I do around here Samantha, and I'm not going to take it anymore!" Pleased with herself, Susan pulled the left side of her mouth into a wicked smile, and exited the washroom, allowing the door to bang shut behind her.

"You're not going to take what anymore, Susan?" Samantha stood at her desk, reviewing a new stack of papers.

"Jesus H...I...I'm not going to take your always stalking me, and scaring the... scaring me...any more," Susan's stammered. Samantha looked at her, seeming unimpressed. "I uh, I have some important information for you."

"So you said, Susan. I got your message."

"I noticed you weren't here this morning." Susan knew the best defense was to be offensive.

"You said that in your message too. I had an early meeting. More to the point, you weren't here this morning. Have another late night? I guess I don't have to ask."

Susan acted out her annoyance by waving the newspaper ad in front of Samantha's face. "I thought you might be interested in a reply they printed."

"Well, of course I am. I placed the ad. Frankly, I'll be glad when this whole thing is behind me." Samantha busied herself with prioritizing her list of urgent calls.

"I *bet* you will."

"Look, Susan, whatever you think you know, this is my personal business, not yours." Samantha's patience seemed especially thin today. "I was under the impression that someone had responded to the ad. Do you have information for me or not?"

"Of course I have *information* for you, Samantha. I always have information for you. I have more information for you than you know what to do with." Susan's voice was rising.

"Well, we got out on the wrong side of the bed, didn't we."

Susan hated it when Samantha was dismissive, and anger made her brave. "My salary doesn't allow me to have a bed, Samantha."

"No, it just allows you to have a full wardrobe of $200 leather outfits."

"Leather is part of my heritage, Samantha. It's what my people wore. I'm carrying on a tradition."

"Oh, you're carrying on a tradition all right...." Samantha stopped herself.

Wounded, Susan asked, "What's that supposed to mean?"

"Never mind, Susan. What about this information?"

Jumping at the chance to get past the stand-off, Susan answered, "Okay, here's what I found out. This woman's name is Stacey Chernak, and she and her husband run a finders agency for long-lost kids."

"Good. Where are they located?"

"Don't know. When I asked for an address and a phone number, all they said was that they'd call back. They said they'd call again at one this afternoon to find out if you were interested in working with them. I said I'd let them know."

"It all sounds rather suspicious."

"You could at least take the phone call from them. There can't be any harm in that."

"Right," Samantha replied sharply. "Be sure to put their call right through to me when it comes in."

"Oh, don't worry. You'll be here at one?"

Samantha regarded her young charge with a wary eye, tired beyond measure of constantly being challenged. "I'll make a point of it," she said firmly.

Samantha could hardly wait to close her door and get some privacy. Dealing with Susan was exhausting. In spite of her constant insolence, Samantha had rules to follow. As a town council appointee, she had to adhere to certain policies, and affirmative action was one of them. There was more to it, though. Much more, after their year and a half together. Samantha had long ago seen through her assistant's tough exterior.

Though she'd never been told what it was, there was some untapped pain behind Susan's rebelliousness—some unresolved issue crying out for healing. This was the real root of the problem. So Sam gave the girl constant opportunities, and made allowances she'd never made for anyone before. *Have I done her any real favors,* Samantha wondered, *or has the kindness been a disservice?*

Suddenly tired, Samantha thought doing some work would be a relief. It wasn't physical fatigue, she knew, but rather deep anxiety that was sapping her strength. Sighing, she opened her office door to retrieve a file just in time to see Susan sling her leather backpack over one shoulder. "Wait just a minute," she called to her. "You're leaving again?"

"I'm going to class." Susan took a beat and smirked at her

mentor. Samantha had signed Susan up for an environmental studies program at Central Coast Community College. It was an hour drive each way and classes lasted an hour and a half. She'd forgotten today was class day. "I never miss school, Samantha, not as long as you're paying."

And with that, Susan sauntered out, leaving Samantha Hugo to handle today's matters of Environmental Planning on her own.

If one place in Milford-Haven escaped the description of "charming" it was Burn It Off, the local exercise establishment. Tucked into the hillside basement of a building it shared with a kitchen supply outlet, a curtain shop, and a hot tub store, it was a white box of a room unrelieved in its stark simplicity. Sally had bought out the previous owner, who'd moved out of town. She'd never had time to advertise it, though, so she was her own best client, with two other regulars—Miranda and Susan.

Mats were piled against a solid wall of mirror, and next to them, a stack of five-inch step platforms. A boom box completed the decor, and Sally bent over to turn it on, stretching as she did. As the loud, rhythmic music started, it masked Sally's groan, and she stood to scowl at herself in the harsh overhead fluorescent lighting.

Sally dragged three of the platforms to positions equally distant from each other, spread out across the small room. "Guess it's just you and me, Girl, and we better get to movin'," she said to herself. She began marching in place, still scowling as she watched her legs jiggle in their hot pink tights.

"Not quite!" Miranda entered the room, tossed her bike helmet on the floor, and peeled off her jacket. Her blue and green leotard and tights accentuated her long, lean lines as she took her place at the platform beside Sally's. "Sorry I'm late!" Miranda shouted over the music.

"Oh, fiddle you're not late, Miranda, I just started a little early. Got to, to catch up with you. Your thighs make me sick!"

"You feel sick?" Miranda was having a hard time hearing over the din.

"Tell ya later!" Sally shouted back, and the two friends smiled at each other in the mirror, marching in place. "One! Two! Three!" she called, holding up fingers. And with that, the two women spun on their sneakers, marched to the back of the room, spun again and marched forward.

It was during one of their backward marches that Susan rounded the corner, flung her backpack, then lovingly placed her leather jacket across it. Her black leotard and tights revealed a thin figure, almost frail. And yet as she began to move she showed a surprising strength, as though her sinews were made of some new grade of steel—thin, but manufactured for endurance. Her hypertensive movements were in sharp contrast to Miranda's fluidity and Sally's bouncing energy.

"Morning, Susan!" called Miranda.

"Hey there, Girl!" Sally shouted.

Susan smiled, not because she was glad to see the others, but because she knew Samantha would be angry if she found *this* was the class she'd run off to attend. Feeling triumphant at getting away with something, she caught the music's rhythm. The three women moved together with a practiced consonance.

"And One...two...lookin' good Girls!" Sally chimed. "Three...four.... Miranda, I don't feel like leadin' today, do you mind?"

Without missing a beat Miranda continued. "No problem. And One...two...three...lift 'em!"

"Lift 'em? Believe me that's all the higher these little legs are gonna go!" Sally called out.

Susan took the instructions literally and performed a kick high enough to hit herself in the head.

"Ooooh-eee that's some extension you got there Girl Friend. I couldn't *never* do that, not even at your age." Sally was beginning to huff and puff as she spoke.

"And over...and turn...and step over, down," continued Miranda. "You do okay, Sally."

"I'll tell you what, if I could kick like that, I know exactly who'd get it and where."

Sally's scowl had returned, and it struck Miranda funny. She began to laugh, determined to keep moving through it. When she could talk she said, "Who's in Sally's dog house this week? Three...four...step together step...."

"Oh, he's gone and done it this time, and he's gonna have to do some kinda fancy foot work to get out of it too. Who does Jack think he is having a kid and not even uh...three...four...letting me know about it?"

This turn in the conversation, such as it was, seemed at last to offer something Susan found interesting. "This is sounding juicy," she called out. "Leading builder in town caught with pants down...."

Miranda threw Susan a disapproving look, which got no notice. Sally was ready to elaborate.

"Oh, he had his pants down all right, even if it was a long long time ago. Uh...uh...two...three...four.... Well, I mean he didn't know about it himself, so I suppose he couldn't really have told me, but at least...uh...three...four...he could have told me that he used to be *married*."

"Why would Jack Sawyer feel an obligation to tell the sordid details of his life to his local breakfast waitress?"

Susan was fishing now, and Miranda knew it was time to

protect her talkative friend. "And V step!" she shouted, "up and over!" The three women were too busy moving now to talk for at least one step-cycle. Despite the complexity of the moves, Sally managed to continue after two minutes.

"I mean who ever heard of being involved with someone...uh...four...and not even *mentioning* such an important little item?"

Susan frowned. "I'm getting lost here. Who's involved with who?"

Miranda spoke up. "Jack's involved with some woman he had a child with. But it was years ago. Keep up Susan. Three...four...."

"Uh...two...uh...three. So. He's all excited about having a kid. So what's so special about a kid you don't even know? Well, I'll show him I can get excited too." Sally was muttering, now, thinking out loud. It didn't prevent Susan from hearing her.

"I bet you can. I gotta get a drink of water." Susan left the room to head for the bottled water holder just outside the door.

Sally continued unabated. "I'll get him excited about a kid he *does* know. A kid who is going to grow up right under his nose. Three...four. And *then* let's see how excited good old Jack can get."

Miranda was getting concerned. While Susan was out of ear shot for a moment,2 she stepped closer to Sally and spoke in as low a voice as she could. "You might want to change the subject Sally, unless you want Susan broadcasting your business around town."

Sally looked at her. "What? Oh. Fiddle. I was gettin' carried away, wasn't I?" Sally walked to the boom box, bent over it, and clicked it off, ejecting the cassette, and inserting another one.

Stepping back into the exercise room, Susan said, "That's it for me." Her voice sounding hollow in the suddenly quiet room, she continued, "I have important things to do. Keep an eye on nasty old Jack, Sally. He certainly has eyes everywhere."

Miranda looked at her carefully. "Is that right, Susan? Does he have ears everywhere too?"

Susan thrust one hip out and stared back at Miranda. Sally now joined Miranda in staring at Susan. Defensively the girl said, "What are you two staring at?"

"Well, moon in the mornin'. You've gone and got yourself a nosering, haven't you?" Sally walked towards her for a closer inspection. "Or is that just a fake one for Halloween?" Sally was next to her by now.

As Sally reached for her, Susan blocked her arm reflexively. "Don't touch!"

"Oh, Lordie, is that sore?"

"Not really," Susan shot back, slinging her backpack across one shoulder. "You *ladies* have a nice day." Susan exited, leaving behind her usual wake of tension.

Miranda and Sally looked at each other, then in silence replaced their step-platforms in orderly stacks and pulled mats to the middle of the floor. Sally pressed the play button and calmer music issued forth.

While they stretched, Miranda wondered how much she could reveal. "You certainly had a lot to say today, Sally."

"You know me, always runnin' off at the mouth."

Miranda was quiet for a moment, leaning into a long stretch to the left. "I don't know Sally. You can keep your lip zipped pretty well when you want to." She paused for a moment. "Which is probably more than I can say for myself."

Sally looked at her friend, just a hint of alarm showing in her expression. "What d' you mean, girl?"

"This started with me, didn't it? What you overheard at your restaurant." Miranda looked chagrined.

"It wasn't you I overheard, Miranda. You know if that

were true I'd o' come talkin' to you first. It was that Samantha I heard. And I do not give a raccoon's tooth for that woman."

They were both silent for a few moments now, Sally feeling fully justified in her actions, Miranda examining her own closely. She knew, now, that Sally had found out about Samantha's child. There was nothing she could do about it, except ask Sally to keep quiet about it. That would only fan the flames, probably. She'd best leave it alone.

Her friend seemed strained. "Was there...was there something else you wanted to tell me Sally?" Miranda waited, looking at Sally in the mirror.

"Oh. Oh, well, that's kind, Miranda, but uh I reckon I said enough already."

Miranda quietly stood and pulled her jacket on over her leotard. "Well, things are not always how they seem, Sally."

"Yeah, I know that, Miranda. I uh, just got some thinkin' to do."

Miranda nodded and left, heading for the outside railing where her bike was waiting. Sally stood and clicked off the tape deck. She looked at herself in the mirror one last time, stuck fingers in her tousled hair, and made a face at herself. Locking the door behind her, she headed back to the restaurant. It was a subdued ending to their usually energizing morning workout.

Chapter 15

Susan closed the door to the public restroom of Milford-Haven's one outdoor restaurant, pulling on the short skirt she'd carried in her backpack. The low, tight leotard top showed just enough skin, and as she walked down Main Street, she felt the dangle of the skull-and-crossbones earrings she'd put on.

She tossed her long, black hair to one side and enjoyed the sound of her Doc Martens as they hit the stairs ascending to the front door of Sawyer Construction. Checking her watch, she noted her professor at CCC would just be handing out this week's test. *What a shame to miss it*, she thought, a smile pulling at her mouth.

The one disadvantage to these shoes was how difficult it was to arrive unannounced. She hated that about Samantha—always sneaking up on her—but for a moment she envied her those soft soles.

Susan pushed open the door and walked as quietly as she could across the expanse of wooden floor. Nothing much happened in this outer office, it seemed. A soiled sofa sat deserted against one wall, and a dog-eared calendar hung askew on the other.

The sound of papers rustling was coming from behind a partially closed door at the far end of the room. Susan paused a moment, then proceeded toward the noise. She peered around the edge of the doorway, and found Kevin looking for something on Jack Sawyer's desk. He was moving quickly, anxiously. Not his usual style.

"Hi there, Kevin." Susan's voice touched off a small explosion in Kevin and his arms jutted out from his body. He dropped the papers he'd been holding, and steadied himself against the large desk.

"Su...Su...."

"Su-san." she finished the word for him.

"Gosh! You...you...."

"Startled you? Gee, Kevin, were you doing something naughty?"

"Wha...what are you doing here?" A touch of anger and defensiveness was making its way through Kevin's stuttering.

"Aren't you glad to see me, Kevin? It makes your job a little easier, doesn't it, keeping an eye on me?" She leaned against Jack's wall, one leg bent, her shoe leaving its mark on the wall's faded paint. It made her seem even shorter compared with his height. She was counting on arousing his protective instincts.

"Gosh darn, how d'you know about that?" Kevin looked genuinely puzzled, and then it gave way to alarm.

In fact, she hadn't known for sure. Now he'd confirmed. it. "So what exactly was your assignment, Kevin? It really doesn't matter if you tell me, right? Now that I know about it?"

Kevin looked both miserable and baffled. "I wasn't supposed to follow you, exactly. This is just...it's my job, Susan. I can't be telling you this stuff.."

"Why not?" Susan persisted.

"I still like you, you know. I hope we can still be friends."

Kevin's voice sounded desperate, and his vulnerability gave her a jones to pounce. "Do you really Kevin? I'm flattered."

She moved toward him, slinging her hips slowly from side to side, the Doc Martens accentuating the movements like drum beats.

Kevin's face got red. "Su- Susan I...I'm just trying to do my job and...and the only stuff you tell me is stuff you'd tell me anyway, stuff you *want* to tell me. I...I don't think it's fair for you to make...make fun of my feelings."

She thrust one hip out. "And your feelings are more important than my privacy, right?"

Kevin stammered, "No...no. Wh...when did you figure it out?"

"It might have been when you followed me into the bookstore. Or it might have been when you tried to follow me down the stairs to exercise class. Or it might have been when you showed up at Wing Ding's." He seemed paralyzed by her rising anger. *Funny how someone so tall can be controlled by someone so small,* she thought. "So, do you think you're inconspicuous? It's like I've had a giant shadow everywhere I move!" She stood so close he had nowhere to go, and nowhere to look but straight down into her tight leotard. She had him now—guilt and a sex sting all at the same time. Softening her tone, she said conspiratorially, "We could make a deal, Kevin."

"A deal? Like...what kind of deal?"

"Like, I don't tell your boss I busted you. And in return, you give *me* information sometimes. You did say you still wanted to be friends, right?"

"I...I don't know. Maybe I make friends too easy," mumbled Kevin.

Susan watched as he rubbed his sweaty palms down his jeans, then she moved a centimeter closer. "We could be really good friends, Kevin."

Kevin looked down at Susan's upturned eyes and shuddered. "I...I don't know if we should be st...standing this close to each other right here in.in...." Susan moved again, her hips pressing the tops of his thighs. A quiet groan issued from his throat.

The outer door of Sawyer Construction banged open. Kevin reacted as though he'd heard a shot, shoving Susan away from him. "Oh, Geez! That must be Jack!" Susan's reactions were quick, and as Kevin shoved, she hooked a finger through his belt, then pulled herself to him again. "Su...Susan!" he pleaded.

Jack loomed in the doorway of his office. "Well, this is cozy. Don't you two have a more private place to carry on your intimacies than in my office?"

"Boss! We weren't...we weren't..."

"Yes, I can see you weren't. I appear to have arrived before you had the chance. Aren't you going to introduce me to your friend?"

Susan stood unperturbed, one hip thrown out, a defiant grin pulling on the left side of her mouth. "I'm Susan Winslow, Mr. Sawyer. But then, you would know that."

"Would I really? I never forget a pretty face."

"I have to get back to work." Susan flashed a smile at Kevin, who blushed. "Mr. Sawyer, good meeting you."

"The pleasure was mine, Ms. Winslow," replied Jack, hiding his surprise behind a stern expression.

With that, Susan's Doc Martens beat a heavy cadence to the door, and the confusion she had stirred hung in the air just as distinctively as did the elixir of her spicy cologne.

Kevin stammered, "Boss, we were just...we were just.... Sorry, Boss."

Jack waved away Kevin's apology. "I don't know how subtle it is to bring her to my office, Kevin. But I knew you understood what I meant by 'keeping tabs' on her. She seems a willing subject. I just hope you can keep up with her."

Chapter 16

Z ack Calvin took a last look around his room at the Belhaven Motel. The carved-wood furniture, the private sitting room and the small fireplace all looked as inviting as they had when he'd arrived. Yet now they looked familiar. A lot could happen in two days.

Feeling only slightly guilty at taking an extra day off, he closed the door and walked along the path beside the planted flower boxes, passed the steam rising from the outdoor hot tub, and headed for his car. Having already checked out, he lifted his black canvas Tumi bag into the Mercedes, closed the trunk and took his seat behind the wheel.

The golden afternoon sunlight made it tempting to stop again at the Cove. But one more walk in its deep sands wouldn't satisfy the longing to stay, and would only make it harder to go.

He pulled out of the Belhaven's parking lot onto Touchstone Beach Road and meandered once more down its length. Otters played just off the rocky shore and a flock of pelicans arced along the coast, a flying chain of beating wings. He crossed the highway at the yellow light and angled the nose of the car up the steep incline. *One more drive by Miranda's, just to be sure I know the way*, he told himself.

The tall pines grew up here, on these narrow uplifts, each hill having its own name. Miranda's was Temescal Hill—he wondered what the derivation might be. Pine needles edged the road, making its borders less distinct. Redwood and stucco homes sat tucked safely behind low fences and hand-crafted signs bore numbers and names. Pumpkins perched by front doors held corn stalks and sunflowers.

The road wound down, around, past a pole house jutting out into thin air, suspended over the hill's sharp decline. An ingenious feat of engineering, he thought. Or else a foolhardy enterprise doomed to catastrophe. Such was the California propensity to build anywhere and everywhere. And here in Milford-Haven, each home rested in the shade of its own trees, and a sense of individuality emanated from each unique structure.

He followed the road up a still-steeper incline and rounded to the right. It leveled here, bordering a ledge where two or three houses were perched in an uneven row. Here it was. Twenty-nine Pine Ridge. He could stop. He could ring the bell, surprise her. Interrupt her work. Say hello. Say good-bye. The car slowed. No. They'd said their good-byes.

The car gently accelerated. He remembered her fatigue-softened face. The car edged over the hill, beginning its descent. He remembered her skin. The Mercedes pulled out onto Highway 1. He remembered their long kiss by her front door.

The road stretched away from Milford-Haven like a long strand of her hair, and Zack pressed the accelerator. He remembered everything about Miranda Jones.

C ynthia'd spent another boring day fulfilling her Junior League duties. This month it was tutoring a derelict high school student who couldn't care less about her studies. Cynthia was hardly qualified for such a task. It wasn't at all what she'd had in mind when offering her services as a volunteer.

Every woman who was anyone in this town had some sort of connection with the Junior League. She'd put on her most conservative suit and marched into their offices—far more humble offices than what she'd expected.

The women were all so earnest, so committed to good works. She wanted to know when the big fund-raisers with plenty of high- rollers and photo opportunities were going to start. In the meanwhile, she was doing her best to put in her time. She wasn't much good at reading, and Jane Eyre struck her as the dullest piece of literature she'd ever encountered. But she'd read for a full hour with the young student. Now she was finally home.

It was just as well she'd had something to distract her. Zack was coming home tonight, and she was anxious. He hadn't called her all weekend. She didn't know what to make of that, so she made nothing of it, choosing, instead, to marshal her resources for a full frontal attack when he got home.

Cynthia tossed her purse onto her bed and impatiently unbuttoned her jacket. Its high neck had restricted her long enough, and the skirt was far too long and shapeless for her taste. She stopped in the bathroom long enough to start a tub of hot suds, then touched the blinking button of her answering machine.

"Cynthia, this is Zelda McIntyre. As you requested, I've made arrangements for the painting you purchased to be shipped directly to the Calvin Estate. Be sure someone is there to receive it, if you don't want the Calvins to rip into the packaging. I must say, dear, I do think it is so generous of you to buy Zackery such a lovely gift. Give me a call. Ta ta."

While the machine was still delivering its final beep, Cynthia was dialing Zelda's office. "Zelda McIntyre." The voice was authoritative, crisp.

"Zelda, this is Cynthia Radcliffe. Thank you so much for going to all this trouble about the painting for Zackery! I really appreciate it."

"Oh, yes, I'm sure you do. I'm afraid I will have to ask for your check, now that shipping arrangements are in place."

"Of course."

"I did the best I could for you, Cynthia, given the special occasion. But I'm afraid the artist does have her bottom line." Zelda's well-practiced negotiating skills were all but wasted on such a willing client.

"Oh, Zelda, I told you that where Zackery is concerned, price is no object. The uh, the artist is a woman did you say?" There was just a hint of alarm in her voice.

"Oh, yes. What better way to match your own sensitivity?"

Cynthia gave a slightly uncomfortable laugh at this. "So. How much is the painting?"

"I was already promised $5,000 by a gallery. But I've reduced it to $3,000. I'd say it's a steal." Zelda refrained from laughing at her own joke.

"Ah!" Cynthia considered the bite this would take out of her portfolio, but this was no time to hesitate, not with the likes of Zelda McIntyre on the line. "That's marvelous. I'll uh...I'll send the check right away. It should be made out to you or to...?"

"To me."

"Three thousand and zero...to Zelda Mc —"

"Cynthia dear, I hate to interrupt, but I must run."

"Oh, fine, Zelda. Thank you again for all your trouble."

"Ta ta!"

Cynthia hung up the phone and sat heavily on the edge of

her white, ruffled bed. This was going to set her back some. At the very least, it would mean one less gown this season. Her investments were doing well, though—well enough to cover an occasional extravagance.

She let her slip fall around her feet and stepped out of it on her way to the tub. The hot water bit into her skin, reddening it under the pillows of white bubbles. *I'm making a big investment in you, Zackery Calvin*, she thought. *You'd better be worth it.*

One hundred miles north, Delmar Johnson sat at his new desk and opened drawers, trying to remember where he'd put his paper clips and hating the thought of adjusting to a new space.

The one saving grace of the move was his new computer. In this one regard, he was rabidly committed to keeping abreast of the times. Were it possible, he'd update software monthly, hardware annually.

But amid the general maelstrom of modern life, Del favored the old over the new. He would sooner un-dent the metal body of a twenty-year-old car than order a new fiberglass bumper; sooner hand-finish a fifty-year-old table than replace it with something freshly veneered.

The same recalcitrance applied to the idea of moving: he hated the very idea. As far as he was concerned, his mother had it right: buy a modest home, treat it with tender loving care, and it would shelter you in good times and bad. Though her house sat empty now, on paper it was still his, still

Work spaces were different. It seemed a useless exercise to form attachments to cubicles and desks, squad rooms and precincts. But somehow when he'd wrenched himself free of Los Angeles, he'd looked for a touchstone, and found it in the old State Police building. Though it's Spanish tile roofs had leaked and its plaster had been in need of repair, it had possessed a magnificence and grace that spoke of noble ideals and the serving of a higher purpose.

Then the County, in its wisdom, had decided to tear it down, constructing a new one on the old site. For months they'd all been displaced to temporary quarters in the basement of the County Courthouse. It was a relief to have sunlight in the workplace again. But the architects hadn't seen fit to incorporate any of the old California glory into the new structure.

Sleek and practical, the new building was reddish brown wood, with desks to match, smelling of new carpet backing and fresh paint. There was a sameness to all the offices, a lack of seasoning to the wood, and a sense that the building was still sitting too high on its foundation, not yet settled in for the duration.

If the walls could talk, they'd have no stories to tell. Not yet.

His mind was wandering, and he brought it back to the papers he was trying to clip together. One was a copy of the notes from his interview of Sally O'Mally about the stranger who'd come to her restaurant looking for Chris Christian. The other was the rendering the police artist had sketched after her recollections.

A man of medium height, of medium build, with medium brown hair, wearing medium-weight glasses. An easy man to miss. And if he happened to be any good at disguises, an impossible man to track. Except that Sally had seen him close-up. And when it came to noticing details about people, Sally O'Mally missed nothing.

The third piece of paper was the court order. Chris Christian had been missing, now, for long enough—over the three-day limit. He knew what he'd have to do when he went to her house.

He knew the detail with which he'd have to go through another person's private world.

Delmar stood and ran a thumb around the inside front of his wide leather belt. It was slightly loose against his taut midriff, but the heavily starched shirt chafed where it connected with the waist. His skin had always been delicate. When he shaved his face, he sometimes raised welts. But he endured this. There was no room for delicacy in this job.

Another 230 miles farther north, CW Jones tossed the day's mail on his desk and sank into his leather chair. Still exerted from his golf game, he tilted his head back to gulp the last of the designer bottled water. When he dropped the spent container into the pewter trash basket, it rang in protest.

Miranda would be horrified I don't recycle, he thought absently. But then, his daughter always had worried about the wrong things.

Reaching for his silver letter opener, CW methodically slit each envelope in the stack of mail, not looking at the return addresses. He paused when he found the postcard. Odd that he'd just been thinking of her and now, here she was. Without reading her message, he turned the card over. The image wasn't half bad this time. At least it wasn't one of her oddly proportioned birds nor was it some ravenous beast.

It seemed a long time now since she'd moved south to one of those silly no-account coastal towns—a place without history or architecture, far below the Bay Area not only geographically, but culturally and financially as well. His mouth twisted at the recognition that her card made the place look almost charming.

If only a fraction of her mother's brains had been passed along to the girl. CW sighed. All the gifts of beauty and grace, poise and brilliance had landed on the other daughter. That Meredith—she was going places. Of that he had no doubt.

But what of poor little Miranda? *Little* was hardly the word, though mercifully she'd managed to lose the baby fat that had plagued her through adolescence. She as sweet enough when she wanted to be, but stubborn as one of the animals she painted—her refusals of sensible jobs as numerous as her failures to win the Duck Stamp prize.

She'd run off to be an artist. Her mother had begged her to reconsider. But after three years, it was obviously a lost cause. What would his old friend Joseph Calvin have to say about her now? Years ago they'd struck that bargain, promising their first-borns would marry. In the beginning it'd been a joke. Then they'd been half-serious. Now it would be a humiliation to imagine foisting his shiftless daughter onto the likes of an accomplished young man like Calvin, Jr. According to the *Wall Street Journal,* he was a rising star in business. No doubt the apple of his father's eye. It was just as well CW'd lost touch with Joseph. He'd just as soon leave well enough alone.

CW turned the postcard over in his hand. "Main Street, Milford-Haven," it said. Looking again at the image he saw blue water, tall trees and quaint buildings. For this, his daughter had given up hearth, home, position and power, everything a good family name could buy.

Miranda's illustration showed a nice enough place to drive through, but you wouldn't want to live there. *What a waste*, he thought. *It'll only upset her mother.*

With a flick of his wrist, he tossed the card into the pewter trash basket, where it barely made a sound.

Chapter 17

Miranda wasn't getting any work done. Since eight in the morning she'd stood in front of her easel, paced the floor, washed her brushes and daydreamed. It was mid-afternoon, and she'd grown tired of the unfinished painting staring back at her.

Grabbing for the metal releases holding up her painting overalls, she let the heavy pants drop to the studio floor, then pulled on her bike pants and headed out the door. She snapped her helmet into place, grabbed the handlebars of her mountain bike, and took off uphill. The exertion of pedaling would be the perfect antidote to her dysfunctional dreaminess.

She stood in the pedals and pumped hard, lowering the gear mechanism still further. This was one thing she loved about biking, that it was hard to think about anything else while doing it. *Right. Left.* She gripped the rounded bar ends she'd had put on her bike recently. They allowed her to pull as she powered herself uphill. Her well-worn gloves felt good gripping the handles. *Right. Left.*

But not even the steep incline could quiet her thoughts. *I've got the Sea Otters to finish, I've got to go by the press to see how the printing of the baby seals lithograph is coming, I have two paintings to ship off to Zelda....* She pedaled even harder, as if strokes of the wheels could remove deadlines.

Topping out on the crest of Upper Pine Ridge, she gulped air as the terrain evened, then lifted her head as her breath came more easily. As she did, the view suddenly took her back to the Cove, and to Zack. "It's your passion." She heard his voice as though he were standing next to her. "You're a natural." She pulled the bike to the edge of the road and looked out through the trees toward the ocean.

He'd been touching the small of her back as he'd spoken to her, looking into her as though her eyes were transparencies, acknowledging her as an artist, as a person, as a woman.

She thought of the solitude she was used to pulling around her like a child's well-worn blanket. It was the solitude that seemed to have holes in it now. She found Zack was with her, even when she was alone. The memory of their embrace at the Cove quickened her pulse.

She fought it, grasping at the tatters of the old solitude-blanket, the only thing she could really call her own. Her beauty, her talent—these were gifts for which she could not claim credit. But her capacity to be alone—this she had carved from her days with stony resolve. And now he'd broken through as though her rock walls were made of water. It was instinctive for him, she knew. *Am I that easy to read? Are all the women he meets?*

She pushed off and stood in the pedals, angling the bike downhill. She resented his intrusion into her private world, yet at the same time, longed for the sweet solace of the company of a man who was an equal. Almost, she could allow that she deserved such a thing in her life.

The wind fluttered her T-shirt as she accelerated downhill. What did the man do for a living? He'd refused to tell her, adeptly changing the subject.

Something to hide. Or was it just that he didn't want to talk about himself? Could we have that much in common?

Miranda tore her chin strap open and grabbed the helmet off her head, tossing it into her bike basket. As she sped down the road, her hair lifted suddenly in the wind, its long tendrils floating behind her, like the thoughts she could not outrun.

By 4 p.m., Zack was passing through Morro Bay. Sunlight hit the wide, flat bay like a klieg light, and it bounced back silver. A tanker stood offshore, and the sight of it was both an intrusion and a welcome back to the real world.

He reached for his cell phone and pressed the auto-dial sequence. The number rang twice before it was answered.

"Hello."

"Hi, Dad, it's me."

"Zack!　Good to hear from you, son. Have a good weekend?"

"Terrific. I can't believe I'd never been to Milford-Haven before. It's so close—but it's another world."

"So that's where you were. Your mother and I used to go up to Milford-Haven. We even took you along once, but you were pretty young."

"Wish I could say I remember it."

"Well, I'm glad you're enjoying yourself. You know we've got some pretty important things to discuss before that meeting with the Coastal Commission next week. I think I've got them convinced that we should be granted that extra offshore lease, but it's going to take the both of us to work this strategy."

"Yeah, Dad. We'll...we'll talk about it. I'm sure there's a

right thing to do, and I'm sure there's a way to do it." Zack could feel the job blasting into his mood like an alarm clock waking him from a delicious dream.

"The only right thing for us is going to be to get those leases. Without them, we're going to see a severe drop in our profit margin for the third quarter."

"Listen, Dad, I'll talk to you about that when I get home."

"And that's just the third quarter. We haven't worked out our final strategies for the fourth quarter, and for that matter —"

"Dad, Dad, I just wanted to check in, and let you know...let you know it's great up there."

After a pause, Joseph spoke again. "What's her name?"

Zack chuckled. "Hey, who said it was a she?"

"Am I wrong?"

It was Zack's turn to pause. "No...no, you're not wrong. So. How's Chris?"

"Don't know." He answered a little too quickly. "She didn't show up the other night. You know how it goes when you date a reporter, though."

"Deadlines?"

"Something like that." Whatever was worrying him, he was keeping it under tight wraps. He changed the subject. "Care to have a bite when you get in?"

"I don't think so, Dad. I want to unpack and get organized for tomorrow morning. Catch you for coffee before the staff meeting?"

"Sounds good, Zack. Drive carefully."

"Always." Zack pressed the "end" button and replaced the handset. The sun was lower now, and California Highway 1 was rejoining the 101 South. Zack looked forward to a quiet evening and a late telephone call to Milford-Haven.

Chapter 18

Joseph replaced the phone in its cradle. Though he felt the call had ended abruptly, he'd learned long ago to let go of such petty annoyances where Zack was concerned. Their friendship—their closeness—meant more to him than that.

Milford-Haven. What memories that brought back! Joan had always loved it there—had begged him to go with her house-hunting. Something small, she'd said, something simple. Some place to escape to—far enough away to keep him out of the immediate reach of the office, and yet not so far that he'd feel he was being irresponsible. "A place to feed the soul," she'd called it. S h e ' d worked with a realtor, slowly, meticulously searching for the perfect place. She'd been nonchalant when she found it—not wanting to overwhelm him with her own enthusiasm. He saw that now, how careful she'd been of his feelings.

But he hadn't seen it then. He'd been angry, belligerent. He'd built her a mansion in Santa Barbara. And it hadn't been enough for her.

She wanted more. Another house. He saw only another drain on energy and resources, a needless expense, a place they'd never use, one more thing to worry about. *Perhaps she'd never wanted the mansion,* he mused. *Perhaps what she'd really wanted all along was a small, simple place.*

The drive home to Santa Barbara that Sunday night was tense and sullen. Joan looked out the window the whole ride, dabbing her eyes with a handkerchief. He tried to explain, and she listened with no reply. He understood only later how deep her disappointment was. Too little too late.

Joseph pushed his large leather chair away from his desk and stood. James was off tonight, and Zack wasn't going to be free for dinner. He'd have to fix himself something. He pulled down on the edges of his cashmere sweater and headed for the kitchen, his shoes clacking on the red Mexican tiles as he passed through the pantry.

On the center island he found a note in James's elegant handwriting: *Mr. C—There's a plate of chicken breasts and fettucini Alfredo prepared in refrigerator B. Place plate in microwave and press reheat, 120°.* James had left him a fully prepared meal. Always so thoughtful. *Also see salad on lower shelf. Dressing in small white pitcher.*

Relieved that dinner was going to be such a simple matter, Joseph still found himself mildly annoyed. Attempting to cook would have kept his mind occupied for at least another hour.

He pressed the prescribed buttons and sat on the nearest rattan-and-wrought-iron barstool, glancing through the carefully stacked array of daily newspapers Joseph had arranged. *Wall Street Journal* on top as always. *Financial Times of London. Barrons. Shipping News. Herald Tribune.* Then the magazines. *The Economist. U.S. News & World Report.* His eye went back to the pink newspaper, which always struck him as an irony—that one of the world's most conservative papers was "pink." Check the old *FT.* See how his friend Jurek was doing. Yup...still U.S. Editor. Check the news on that oil spill...yes, here it was....

Milford Haven, Wales: The Liberian-flagged, Russian-crewed 147,000 ton oil tanker, *Sea Empress* grounded on the rocks in the mouth of Milford Haven. In the six days it has required to free the tanker, 73,450 tons of oil have leaked from the tanker. This is the third largest oil spill to have occurred in UK waters.

Another Milford Haven...ironic that this should happen today. He wondered if the Welsh town was as beautiful and pristine as its California counterpart—a fact that would make the spill all the more tragic. He thought suddenly of one of his own tankers caught on rocks, fouling the coastline, and shuddered. His bad mood worsening, he put down the unfinished paper and returned to the carefully arranged kitchen counter.

Looking at the tray James had left out for him—preset with flatware, plate and glass—he waited for the microwave to beep. Then he placed the steaming food on the fine china, poured himself a short glass of Chablis, and headed for the large comfortable den adjoining the kitchen. It'd been Joan's design—a way of staying connected with the family while she cooked. She'd been a superb cook, a *Cordon Bleu* chef. She'd taught James well.

Joseph clicked the TV remote and watched absently as the CNN reporter held forth on matters of interest in Tel Aviv. He switched to Chris's station. *If I can't see the woman in person, I can at least see her on the box,* he thought. "Local news is next," announced the unseen voice. He took several bites while the endless local commercials scrolled through. "So unprofessionally pro-duced," Chris always complained. "If they're spending all this money on the media buy, why in blazes don't they hire decent advertising firms?" A pet peeve.

Joseph took a swallow of Chablis and refocused as the news began. There he was, Chris's co-anchor. *Handsome devil,*

Joseph thought, with a twinge of jealousy.

"Nothing animates the face," Chris had reassured him. "He's not a real reporter—just a talking head."

"...and Chris Christian has the night off."

Joseph sat up straight. *The night off? What the hell?* The woman was obviously seeing someone else and hadn't the nerve to tell him. Joseph put his tray aside and strode away from the TV, the co-anchor still reporting local events. Joseph began to pace. He should've known better than ever to begin dating a younger woman.

What's the matter with you? he chided himself. *You're a fool! All that talk about deadlines and crazy schedules...she was setting you up, idiot! Trying to cushion you, knowing there'd be a fall.*

Joseph took his tray into the kitchen and restrained himself from hurling his plate into the stainless steel sink. *Damn!* It wasn't worth feeling excited by some young thing if this kind of stress and upset came with the package.

He considered his options: pour himself a stiff drink; jump into his car and roar up the highway; write Chris a curt letter; lay low.

He chose the latter. Now the challenge was to peel himself off the ceiling; calm himself down; refocus on work, house, charity events, all the tasks and responsibilities cluttering his agenda book.

Walking into his office, he slammed the door and yanked the chair from under his desk. Staring at his brown leather agenda, he flipped it open and glanced at the pages full of meetings, notes, lists, phone calls.

He reread tomorrow's schedule—a habit he'd cultivated years ago as a means of preparing himself for the next business day. Automatically he reran the facts and background on the people with whom he'd be meeting, prioritized which items on his desk needed his attention first. He felt calmer now. He sat down. He flipped to the previous day, reviewing what he'd done, the calls he'd made and received.

And then he began leafing methodically backwards, slowly reviewing the past several days, until he came to his brief memo. *Dinner with Chris*, it said. Seemed innocuous enough. Important enough for him to write it down. Not important enough for her to show up. He turned back still further. Three days before that had been their last date.

Chris was all that was written. But he knew his own shorthand. The word was written at an angle. He never did that with business appointments. *How transparent my feelings are*, he thought bitterly. He passed his finger across the word written such a short time ago.

What had happened that night? Oh, yes. He smiled in spite of himself. And waking up with her was always a disconcerting and pleasurable surprise. Then she'd received that phone call... something about going to a house if she wanted the story. He'd made light of the mysteriously obscure message. But she hadn't. She'd suddenly turned all business.

Well, I can do the same, he thought. He stood and slammed the agenda closed with a finality he was surprised he could summon so suddenly.

Samantha paced in her cramped living room. Having waited at the office for the three o'clock phone call that never came, she'd finally left for home. Now at four, the Art Nouveau clock rang out the hour, and again she was amazed at how another sixty minutes had flown by. Worse than that, she had nothing productive to show for it, and she could ill afford to waste what precious time she had away from the office.

She had no idea how to handle these feelings. She'd thought they were processed long ago and was nothing short of amazed at how they took her attention now. She had no choice but to reckon with them somehow.

At one end of her short walk, the kitchen counter serving as her desk seemed to groan under the weight of papers and files stacked too high to remain secure. She regarded the piles distastefully and walked to her refrigerator, opening it and looking over its contents. A half- eaten apple. The remnants of a salad. A head of red cabbage. Four bottles of cranberry juice. Two yogurts.

She slammed the door, badly rattling the contents of the refrigerator door. Wincing, she knew there was only one place she could go in a mood like this.

She'd open her journal and write and write till either her hand cramped and the damp sea air chilled her to the bone, or the sunlight failed—whichever came first.

Walking quickly to her bedroom, she pulled on her heavy cableknit sweater and picked up the latest in a series of cloth-covered, oversized journals in which she wrote almost daily.

With a combination of relief and defiance, she grabbed her shoulder bag and walked out her front door. Situating herself behind the wheel of her car, she slammed the door of her Jeep Cherokee, turned her key in the ignition, and started for the Cove.

Chapter 19

A full harvest moon shined its face in a black sky, hiding the stars with its brilliance and piercing wraiths of cloud with iridescent gold. Although Halloween was only days away, the spirits of the Central Coast seemed more inclined to bless than to terrify.

Miranda soaked longer than usual in an exceptionally hot tub after her long bike ride. Despite having treated her muscles brutally, they ached with only a mild throb. The steaming water covered her shoulders and grazed her chin, misting the window through which she could usually see the stars. She closed her eyes and enjoyed one more long, delicious moment before forcing herself to move, and it was only the fear of falling asleep and sliding down under the surface that inspired her climb out.

She stood, surging from the water, the sound loud after the quiet. *Like a whale breaching*, she thought. She dried herself and brushed her long hair slowly, the bristles scraping pleasantly along her scalp. From a hook on the wall she pulled a full-length nightshirt of undyed cotton and felt it float comfortable over her warm skin. *What does Zack wear to bed?* she wondered.

When she'd brushed her teeth, she slid into slippers and

shuffled down the hall. So often she'd climb the stairs to the studio for a final look at a canvas. She'd wake herself and end up working all night. Not tonight. It wasn't even a temptation.

She walked into her bedroom and paused for a moment, looking out the large window. Stars blinked through the tops of the tall pines standing adjacent to the house. An owl hooted. She smiled, comforted by the sound, as though the world was telling her good night.

She lifted a corner of her down comforter and slid between the sheets. *I wonder what you're thinking, Zack Calvin?* And with a pleasant exhaustion, Miranda sank into a deep sleep.

*Z*ack stood in his shower, supporting his weight with his outstretched arms, letting the hot needles of water hammer his tired shoulders. There was nothing particularly good about being back home, except for the shower. He'd dropped his bags, thrown off his clothes and stepped into the spacious glassed cubicle immediately.

He pictured Miranda being here with him, her long hair streaming with water, clinging to her body. The thought aroused him, and he stopped himself from carrying it further, for now. *Let the relationship keep up with itself for once*, he thought. It was a goal. A challenge. *One I've never achieved before, God knows.*

Turning the handle to the off position, Zack saw the stack of freshly laundered, oversized bath sheets James always left in his bathroom. He used the top one—huge, white, and fragrant—to scrub the excess water from his hair, then wrapped it around his waist.

Slightly overheated from the shower, he flopped onto his

bed and clicked the TV remote. He knew he wouldn't watch long...just something to help him decompress after the drive. Enjoying the temporary mindlessness, he channel-surfed for a few minutes. He glanced at his clock. He'd wanted to call Miranda tonight, but he had hesitated, and now it was late. He was afraid he'd wake her. *Tomorrow,* he thought. *Tomorrow I'll call her.* He smiled as he thought of her face, wonderful in its natural beauty. *A find*, he thought. *A real find.*

Zack clicked off the TV. Standing, he turned off all the bedroom lights, and dropped his towel. He returned to the bathroom for a moment, grabbing a litre bottle of Evian water from the supply beneath his sink.

In a minute, he was back in the bedroom. Turning down the charcoal-gray bed covers, he paused to inhale a trace of gardenia. *Must be wafting in through the window,* he thought. His eyes hadn't adjusted to the dark, but he knew the feel of the bed as well as he knew his own hand. *I'm going to sleep well tonight*, he thought.

In the next second, his heart nearly jumped out of his chest, and his body leapt out of the bed. "Holy Mother of God!" He'd somehow managed to land on his feet. His heart hammered his ribs like a blacksmith working on an anvil.

"No, no, Zackery. It's just Cynthia."

Her voice came out of the dark, disembodied. *This has to be a practical joke,* he thought. *Someone's put a tape recorder on my bed and had wired it to a sensor.*

Zack snapped on the light beside his bed. "What the hell...Cynthia? What do you think you're doing?"

There she was, as picture perfect as a catalogue girl, draped in something pink and satin, and perfectly posed, one leg coyly perched on top of the covers, the bed clothes concealing the rest of her. He continued to stand dumbfounded.

"That's quite a picture, Zackery darling. I've always thought that was your best outfit."

Only then did he remember he was standing naked. He cursed again and grabbed behind his bathroom door for a robe.

"Cynthia...what...how did you get in here?"

"Oh, Zackery, please, we're practically engaged."

He let out a loud guffaw. "What ever gave you the idea we were engaged, Cynthia? Is this one of your friends' ideas, or did it come to you in a private vision?"

With sudden modesty, she pulled the covers up a little higher. "Oh, Zackery, you know me, I can't resist a little shock value."

"Yeah, well, you can say that again. I don't think my heart's going to slow down till Tuesday." Zack sat heavily on the edge of the bed, the adrenalin rush subsiding, leaving him drained.

She slid closer to him. "Zackery...you know I didn't mean anything by it! I just mean that you're...I missed you so much!" Before he could defend himself, she planted her lips on his, pressing her warm, pulsing body against him. She kissed him passionately, expertly.

Coming up for air, he heard her whisper words between the next round of kisses. "I was thinking about you last night," she said, her breath shallow, her voice a guttural stage whisper. "I was thinking about the way you—"

"Yeah. I...I missed you too." He pushed her away, gently, his guilt diminishing his anger. "I uh, listen, why don't you..."

"Oh, yes! Zackery, yes! I will!" She was on him again in an instant, her fragrant blond curls wrapping around his face, the pink satin reaching his bare chest. Leaning against him, she pushed him down into the pillows.

"I...Cynthia...there's...." He tried to protest.

"I know darling, I know. You're tired. You've had a long

drive. Don't worry. Cynthia fix."

As he tried to frame words, Zack heard a snap, and Cynthia's breasts tumbled out of the satin. He lay there speechless as he felt her knees grip either side of his hips.

Why was it that he felt so helpless? She was arousing him in spite of himself. "Ooohh. So you did miss me." She moved again, and he felt himself responding.

Why couldn't he say that everything had changed now, that he'd met himself somewhere on that highway north, that somewhere a window had opened? Or had it really? Had the weekend been just a dream? And was this his rude awakening back in the real world?

"Oh, oh, Zackery, you're so good to me." The passion in her voice was intoxicating. Cynthia leaned into him now, riding him with expertise both brutal and compelling in its familiarity.

And despite his best intentions, Zack found he had no choice but to satisfy the rapacious appetite of the hungriest woman he knew.

Chapter 20

from Samantha Hugo's Journal
written at the Cove

There's a woman in the post office I don't know well, but often see. When she saw me carrying my journal, she asked if I wrote in it every day. No, I said, but often. Oh, brother, she said, I could fill it up for you. We laughed, but I sensed her pain.

She launched into an abbreviated version of her story—that she'd been hurt by a man. In her head, she knew he was no good for her. But her heart just said, So what? So she lives with this division between the logical and the intuitive sides of herself. It was the same with all her women friends, she said. They'd all decided men were hopelessly stupid and callous about feelings.

Thinking about her afterward, this seemed sad. Not that I don't agree men can be stupid—it's amazing how often I think that about Jack! But as women, we're not doing a good job either, if we're relegating our intuitions to hopelessly romantic flutterings that cannot inform our choices or infuse us with courage to know what we feel and say what we need.

The linear knowledge of the head can be so vital. In

meetings, sometimes, I've seen men cut through a morass of details and get right to the issue with a clarity I wish I had ability. I've seen Lorraine chair the Town Council meetings with that same straight-line approach, so it's not always a gender issue. But I must admit—sometimes grudgingly—men make the world a better place by providing clarity and focus.

Equally important is the contextual, circular knowledge of the heart—often the purview of women. I'm beginning to wonder if the heart isn't just as much a thinking organ as the brain. It knows so much, yet its information isn't presented in verbiage. Have we lost its language? Is that why we can't hear what the heart is trying to tell us? We hear something, but dismiss it as "foolish" or "hopelessly romantic" or "sentimental." That minimizes its true import.

Maybe it's because of the noticeable absence of a man in my life, but for so long I've ignored the heart and been governed by the head. I've made a practice of it, dismissing my feelings as immature vestiges of sentimentality. But all along, the heart has been ticking, and—perhaps more important— knowing. Now it's made its presence known with an unmistakable depth of emotion far beyond something I can relegate or control.

The anguish of losing a child no one can know but the parent who has suffered the loss. I wouldn't have believed that thirty years ago. I thought I knew all about loss then.

For years I thought I did a good job overcoming that dark chapter. The river was turbulent for me in those days, spilling its banks and doing damage in ways I had no way of understanding. Maybe that's the way it is for every 20-year-old. Maybe it's the function of the elders to clean up those muddy floods, right those boats, send the fledgling adults more steadily down river.

But what of the little passenger I failed to protect? I comfort myself that I was immature. But was I really? I was a college student, so worldly-wise in matters of anthropology...so instinct-injured when it came to matters of the heart.

I bore a child, flesh of my flesh, blood of my blood. No, I didn't drown him. But I placed him ashore. I trusted to the kindness of strangers that he would be cared for in some appropriate way.

As the years went by, I comforted myself that this mistake had long since washed itself to the sea with the volume of my tears. But such was not the case. The coldness with which I accepted the reality that I was not prepared to rear a child froze my heart one day when I wasn't looking. Only now has the thaw begun.

Chilling thought. Cold comfort.

Perhaps I've only managed the loss as one manages a chronic disease with the right prescription. It seems my prescription has run out, and now the loss is hitting me with a force I could not have imagined.

It's beginning to color how I look at Jack. That's another thing I thought was washed out to sea decades ago—the passion I had for that man. Now I'm not so sure. When I'm screaming at him about environmental regulations, I want to yell, "I've lost our son!" I even want to shout at him, "Comfort me! Put your arms around me!" And yet the secret is locked, and I can't find the key. Not even my bitterness is a strong enough acid to burn through the lock I turned so many years ago.

Images are beginning to surface like photographs being developed from a lost roll of film. To see again that child-face bursting with curiosity, trusting his entire child-heart to his only known ally, venturing his tiny boat upon the big waters of life—without me.

Abandonment is looming large in my vocabulary these days. The Latin "bandon" means jurisdiction, and the definition in my old Websters is fearsome: "To give up with the intent of

never again claiming one's rights or interests in; to desert."
Possibly the second meaning is even worse: "To give oneself up
without attempt at self-control, as to grief."

    What did I do to the child psyche? Without the orienting
beacon of a mother's presence, did it struggle to feel whole as he
grew? Was the memory of loss buried, and did it decay and fade
away? Did he become strong and independent? Or did he merely
manage as I did, and will the secret engulf him one day in a flood
of self-doubt and conflicted feelings?

    If I find him and reveal myself as his mother—do I do him
a kindness, resolving the riddle of his life? Or do I destroy his
world, smash his trust in all that he has known? Do I have to wait
to be found in order to protect his child-heart still? If so, do I
leave clues like small piles of rocks for him to follow?

    Can I function while this boils within me? My one enemy
in life is Jack. Do I go to him and ask for leniency? Forgiveness?
Understanding? Compassion? Didn't he bury these qualities long
ago? Isn't that why I left him?

    But can I get through this alone? Can I get through it at
all?

    My heart is restless and I know I'm looking for
something. It's not geographic—I know I've found a home here in
this special town. But the restlessness is tangible, and I feel the
need to find my son as a physical yearning. It's also psychological,
in that I sense a discomfort that always signifies growth. It's as
though I've been told there's a treasure buried somewhere and I
know I'm looking for the map. Dostoyevsky says, "Only the heart
knows how to find what is precious."

    Some days I look at my life and by and large it's a happy
one. I'm busy, productive. I passionately care about my work. I
believe I'm doing what I was put here in this world to do. Or at
least I did believe that until now.

I've built something in Milford-Haven. Some people dislike me, but at the end of the day they know what I stand for, and they respect that. Well, everyone but Jack respects it, and I discount his publicly poor opinion of me as a matter of private vanity.

Though I tell myself I don't care what other people think, I imagine it would be painful if the small-town gossip mill got hold of this. "Samantha—who claims to have such a high moral tone, who fell from grace even as she stumbled into adulthood. Samantha—the Town Council member who years ago gave up a child for adoption...Samantha—the unfit mother." They'd enjoy chewing me up and spitting me out at breakfast for at least a few weeks.

More than caring what others think, I care about making sense of my life. I care that the events and choices of my life be logical, that I can trace a path of reason—even if no one else can.

In the Myers Briggs Personality Type Indicator, there are Sensors and Feelers. A Sensor is the classic "show me" type: he trusts only what he can see, touch, hear and taste. A thing isn't entirely real to him unless it's standing in front of him. In fact, that's his definition of "tangible."

A Feeler is just the opposite—and it describes me perfectly. I trust what I feel, even if all the external evidence is against it. You can show me a bridge, but if it "feels" wrong, I won't cross it; show me a report signed, sealed and delivered, but if I sense something phony about it, I'll dismiss it. I have to go with my heart.

The physical way of looking at the heart is the only one validated by our society. From this perspective the heart is an organ that beats about 100,000 times in a day, thirty-five million times in a year, and more than two-and-a-half billion times in a lifetime. It's the pump that moves a million barrels of blood during its hundred-year run—enough to fill more than three super tankers.

But Deepak Chopra—ignored by some, revered by others—says something far more significant. He says the heart is the "invisible organizing power of the universe."

That got me thinking metaphorically: when we talk about the "heart of the matter" we're talking about the core issue; to "take heart" is to be courageous; to be "soft-hearted" is to have compassion and mercy; one's "hearthrob" is the love of one's life; "heartache" is misery; "heartbreak" is wretched disappointment; to "hearten" is to reassure; and a "heartfelt" sentiment is a badge of authenticity.

I agree with Chopra when he says that the power at the core of any developing idea is what causes it to manifest. I'm sure I'm experiencing this phenomenon right now as a kind of inner guidance system I can't explain, and can't avoid.

And yet I keep these instincts to myself, for they are not acceptable in our logic-dominated society. I find myself searching for ways to back my intuitive findings with some kind of empirical documentation lest I myself be dismissed as a well-meaning anecdote-toting tree-hugger rather than a serious scientist.

I think, however, that the only way to survive this chapter of my personal life is to trust the heart more than the head, because the heart is contextual where the head is linear. Somehow the heart is silently knowing, while the head is frantically wondering.

It's going to take more than brains to get through this. It's going to take heart, soul, faith, guts, maybe even luck—whatever that is.

After all these years, this one thing I know:

What matters is not what gossip reports, nor what reason suspects, but what the heart knows.

Cast of Characters

Joseph Calvin: late 50s, 6'1, handsome, lean, gray eyes, steel-gray hair, clean-shaven; CEO of Santa Barbara's Calvin Oil; highly eligible widower; dates Chris Christian.

Zackery Calvin: mid 30s, 6'2, blue eyes, handsome, lean, athletic, dark blond hair; Vice President of Calvin Oil, works with his father; most eligible Santa Barbara ladies' man; dates Cynthia; smitten by Miranda.

Nicole Champagne: mid 20s, 5'5, chic, sleek, brunette; runs Milford-Haven's "Finders' Gallery"; sells Miranda's and other artists' work with skill; originally from Montreal, Quebec.

Stacey Chernak: 49, 5'6, blue eyes, blond, sweet, deeper than she seems, submissive, speaks with a Swiss accent; works with her abusive husband at the Chernak Agency, and works full time for Clarke Shipping.

Wilhelm Chernak: 64, 6', black deepset eyes, salt-and-pepper hair, deep resonant voice, a Swiss citizen who still carries an accent from his native Germany; capable of fierce and sudden anger; started the Chernak Agency, a service for finding missing children; abuses his wife Stacey.

Chris Christian: early 40s, 5'6, blond, vivacious, beautiful, intense; Santa Barbara KSB-TV weekend news anchor and special reporter; lives in Santa Maria; dates Joseph Calvin.

Russell Clarke: Businessman who commissions Jack Sawyer to build him Milford-Haven's most magnificent seaside house.

Samantha Hugo: early 50s, 5'9, brown eyes, statuesque redhead; Director of Milford-Haven's Environmental Planning Commission; Miranda's friend; Jack Sawyer's former wife; a journal writer.

Deputy Delmar Johnson: early 30s, 6'2, brown eyes, black hair, handsome, muscular, African-American; with the San Luis Obispo County Sheriff's Department, assigned to the Special Projects Unit; originally from South Central Los Angeles.

Miranda Jones: early 30s, 5'9, beautiful, lean, athletic, green eyes, long brunette hair; Milford-Haven artist; a staunch environmentalist whose paintings depict endangered species.

Mr. Man: age unknown, medium height, medium build; one of reporter Chris Christian's anonymous sources.

Zelda McIntyre: 50, 5'1, violet eyes, black hair, voluptuous, dramatic and striking; Santa Barbara corporate art buyer; Miranda's artist's rep; has designs on Joseph Calvin.

Sally O'Mally: early 40s, 5'3, perfectly proportioned, blond curly hair; owner of Milford-Haven's restaurant *Sally's*; originally from Arkansas; Miranda's friend; secretly involved with Jack Sawyer.

Cynthia Radcliffe: early 30s, 5'8, shapely, gorgeous, blond; Santa Barbara social climber; Zackery's girlfriend.

Kevin Ransom: late 20s, 6'8, sandy hair, strong jaw line, lean, muscular without effort; works for Jack at Sawyer Construction; innocent, naive, kind; has longings for Susan Winslow.

Jack Sawyer: mid-50s, 6', blue eyes, salt-and-pepper hair, barrel-chested, solidly muscular, ruggedly handsome; Milford-Haven contractor/builder; Samantha Hugo's former husband; secretly involved with Sally O'Mally.

Susan Winslow: mid-20s, 5'4, brown eyes, long black hair, attractive but sullen, Native American; Samantha's secretary at the EPC; feels trapped in Milford-Haven; ambivalent about her heritage; toys with Kevin.

Return soon to...
Milford-Haven!

Here's an excerpt from the
Prologue of

Mara Purl's

Closer Than You Think

Book Two
in the exciting Milford-Haven series

Prologue

Senior Deputy Delmar Johnson had stayed too long in his office and now it had grown dark. The days had grown short and winter rains had again doused the Central Coast much of the day. Highway 1 stretched past the window, a slick ribbon of asphalt devoid of traffic, and he couldn't shake his feeling of foreboding.

Chris Christian was definitely missing, and Del had been without a clue as to where to begin his search. The call from Detective Rogers hadn't been a break in the case, exactly, but at least it would be a starting point. A Mr. J. Calvin of Santa Barbara had reported her missing, and had asked that Captain Sandoval assign the matter personally. Keep it quiet, he had apparently said. He'd cooperate fully. The Captain had called Rogers. Rogers had wanted Del in on the interview.

It'd been only two months since Del made senior deputy, and he appreciated the vote of confidence from the Captain—if, in fact, that's what it was. They'd been short-handed, leaving a slot open for someone who happened to be in the right place at the right time. But it was always hard to tell, when you were the new kid on the block, if a new assignment meant you were being given a chance, or being thrown to the dogs.

He'd done his one-year probation with the Sheriff's department in San Luis Obispo County, and had spent it on patrol in all three sub-stations: Templeton to the north, Los Osos in the middle, and Arroyo Grande, which encompassed everything south to the Santa Barbara County line. Among other things, the year of patrol work meant he'd learned a lot about the area—enough to know he loved the Central Coast.

The California Department of Forestry had a new building in Milford-Haven. At first they'd been willing only to allow the use of a desk and phone. But when they'd learned of Del's computer expertise, and found out he had his own system, they'd become a lot friendlier. Now he shared space provided by the CDF, and his new office suited him down to the ground.

By any standards his promotion had come quickly—quickly enough to cause some resentment. But that didn't worry Del. His five years with the L.A.P.D. on the streets of South Central had prepared him as few officers are ever prepared. Now he'd been assigned to SPU—Special Problems Unit. It had the potential to be the ideal job. He answered only to the Captain, and was assigned to work with detectives—or anyone else—when needed. In this unit, there was no case load, per se. The idea was to keep its members free to respond as needed. So he'd earned the title Senior Deputy Johnson, more responsibility, and more freedom than he'd had in his professional life. An enormous vote of confidence. Or not.

Del considered again the particulars of the meeting with Joseph Calvin. It was to take place after-hours, when they couldn't be observed. They were to meet at his private residence. The butler would have retired for the evening: Calvin himself would answer the door. Did this mean that a member of the white bastion of Santa Barbara society was embarrassed at being questioned by a black deputy? Del wasn't prepared to rule out the racial persuasion, despite all reassurances to the contrary. He'd been told he was to arrive at 10 pm. It was time to go.

Del headed for his car. His keys jangled as they hit his taut hips, making a rhythmic music with his boots as they thudded through the corridor and down the stairs. Like a one-man percussion section echoing through the deserted building, he filled the hallways with his sound, then emptied them abruptly with a final clang of the double front doors. Making sure the building was locked, he pressed his car alarm button, its mechanical chirp still an uncommon sound on the Central Coast.

Another perk of the SPU job was access to four-by-four vehicles. The Suburban coughed into activity and settled into a deep, growling purr as it gathered speed. It sometimes seemed to Del nothing short of miraculous that such an expanse of road as Highway 1 could be as safe and clear as it was. The mean streets of his own childhood sometimes rose out of the dark to haunt him. If a car backfired, he always assumed first it was a shot, his body reflexively tensing, his senses coming to full alert. Even after twenty-six months, he had not yet unlearned those inner city reactions. Perhaps, he thought as the Suburban ate up miles, he never would. Indeed, perhaps he never should.

Del had kept his radio on low volume. Halfway to his destination, he heard, "Twenty-four-Z-four."

"Z-four," he answered quickly. He'd been the last the join the four-person SPU unit, and that had given him the number "four."

"Ten-twenty-one as soon as possible."

"Ten four."

Ten-twenty-one meant "call home." Twenty-four was the number for the main station at San Luis. As Del used his cell phone to place the call, he wondered who needed to speak with him in enough detail that the radio couldn't be used.

"Dispatch," the sheriff's office answered.

"This is Johnson."

"I'll put you through."   The night sped by outside the Suburban, and Del watched the road. Zebra was the code name for the SPU unit. Well, we are a bunch of wild animals. He chuckled to himself, and got serious as someone came back on the line.

"Johnson, this is Rogers. I'm sorry to give you such short notice, but you're going to have to handle the Calvin interview on your own."

"Oh?"

"I know, irregular procedure, but we're short-handed tonight, and we've got a situation over on the 101. No way I'll get to Santa Barbara in time."

"Should I cancel? Explain to Mr. Calvin that you could see him tomorrow?"

"No, that would only make matters worse. I don't know what's so urgent, but the word came down from the top that someone should speak to him tonight. Who knows, maybe he'll be impressed by a suit ringing his doorbell at 10 pm."

Del glanced at his sleeve. He wasn't wearing a suit. "Anything in particular I should ask him?"

"No, you know what to do. Standard stuff—missing person report. Just keep it simple. Fill me in first thing tomorrow."

"Will do."   Del closed his cell phone and kept his foot steady on the accelerator. Mr. Calvin was in for a little surprise this evening. Del was anxious to gauge his reaction.

Milford-Haven

The Continuing Novels
by Mara Purl

Find yourself in...

Milford-Haven
The little town with big stories...
Small town simplicities...Global complexities

www.milfordhaven.com

Where Jack, Zack, Miranda, Cornelius, Samantha, Rune, Meredith, Connie, Emily, Kevin, Joseph, Sally, Tony, Zelda, Notes, Susan, and Cynthia, are building, buying, painting, observing, planning, rehearsing, advising, traveling, reporting, cogitating, dominating, dishing, dealing, conniving, playing, sneaking, and seducing, respectively.

The radio drama, the novels, the web site, the audio books

Milford-Haven Enterprises

PO Box 7304-629   818-762-2945 phone
North Hollywood, CA 91603   818-508-0299 FAX
                     Milfordhaven@aol.com

Now that you've visited
Milford-Haven
in your imagination...
Visit the region
for <u>real</u>!

California's Central Coast
awaits!

Enjoy special offers
from these fine businesses...

THANK YOU
to the following individuals
and organizations
who generously provided
special bonus gifts to my readers
during the Internet Launches of
What the Heart Knows:

The Chopra Center
www.chopra.com

Katherine Shirek Doughtie
www.aphroditeinjeans.com

Erin Gray
www.eringray.com

Marilyn Harris
www.marilynharris.com

Mary Helsaple
www.helsaple.com

Linda Purl
www.lindapurl.net

Linda Seger
www.lindaseger.com

Discover

Haven Books

www.havenbooks.net

Fiction with vision.
Non-fiction with purpose.

Make Your Reading a Haven!

Audio Books
Audio Dramas

Make Your Listening a Haven!

Haven Books
10153 ½ Riverside Drive, North Hollywood, CA 91602
818/ 503-2518 phone   818/ 508-0299 FAX
info@havenbooks.net

Mara Purl is an award-winning writer-producer-performer. Her world of *Milford-Haven* has now expanded into a series of popular novels and short stories. The beloved fictitious town first appeared in Mara's *Milford-Haven, U.S.A.* ©, the first American radio drama ever licensed and broadcast by the BBC where it reached an audience of 4.5 million listeners throughout the U.K. and the show is currently on the air in the U.S.

Milford-Haven won the Finalist Award at the 1994 New York Festivals International Radio Competition. New York's Museum of Television & Radio and Chicago's Museum of Broadcast Communications have placed all broadcast episodes of the show into their permanent archive collections.

Mara's writing credits include plays, screenplays, scripts for *Guiding Light*, cover stories for *Rolling Stone*, staff writing with the *Financial Times (of London)*, and the Associated Press. She is the co-author (with Erin Gray) of *Act Right*. Mara is the Founder of S.T.A.R. – Student Theatre And Radio, a program she has taught for ten years in three states.

As an actress, Mara was "Darla Cook" on *Days Of Our Lives*, and she performs *Mary Shelley - In Her Own Words*, winner of the 2003 Peak Award. Mara grew up in Tokyo, Japan, and earned a performing and literary degree from Bennington College. Mara was named one of twelve Women of the Year 2002 by the Los Angeles County Commission for Women.

She is married to Dr. Larry Norfleet, and lives in Los Angeles, California, and in Colorado Springs, Colorado.